JAY TINSIANO AND JAY NEWTON

Blood Cull

Acknowledgement

We would like to thank all our beta readers especially Lynn Hallbrooks, Judylynn Gries and Tony Crewe.

Chapter 1

His muscles burned with the effort, yet there could be no stopping now. Joel Hopkins drew in sharp, ragged breaths as the adrenaline coursed through his body.

He glanced behind but couldn't see anything, yet he knew his pursuer was there. Forcing his exhausted muscles on, he grunted, the primitive sound spliced with fear.-

The dark woodland was quiet, just the thud of his bare feet on the woodland ground, the cracking of deadwood, and his thumping heart in his ears. Joel Hopkins was running as fast as he physically could, passing flashes of green bushes and the blur of trees through wet, terrified eyes.

In his left hand, he clutched a small knife. How or why he had it, he did not know, but his pursuer must have given it to him. It felt useless, pointless to have. His pursuer moved unseen somewhere behind him, edging closer like his own shadow. Still, he clung to the blade as if it was a lifeline.

Then his foot caught on an unseen root. He stumbled forward, falling hard on the ground. Joel groaned out loud, quickly turning his head to look behind through the dense woods. Moonlight cast an eerie greenish hue through the canopies that caused mottled patterns on the ground. For a brief moment, he caught the smell of wild garlic and bluebells. It was as if nature was reminding him of reasons to live.

Joel tried to slow his breathing, attempting to gain some control. He wasn't used to this. He was usually the one calling the shots, telling people how it was.

He desperately tried to calm himself. To listen.

A slow wind moved through the trees. Had he lost the pursuer? Joel felt a slither of hope.

Perhaps he had?

He gazed down at his Armani jacket sleeve for a moment, ripped and smeared with mud.

The silence was almost peaceful, then there was a crack from dead-wood being broken somewhere in the distance. Joel's stomach lurched with dread. He looked around and realised the knife he had been clutching was gone and nowhere in sight. He crawled along the ground to a nearby oak tree, circling around the thick base and hid in its shadow. Now he waited, listening, barely able to breathe.

Several hours earlier, he had come back home from work. Still, in his suit, he took a gin and tonic onto his patio that overlooked his immaculate garden.

Claudia, his wife of twenty years, was visiting a friend and with his only daughter out of town, it felt great to have the house to himself. He sat down to read, devouring his property investment magazines and then moved onto *International Living* to immerse himself in opportunities abroad. His property conveyancing firm had recorded one of their best years ever, and a massive bonus was assured. Joel was smart enough not to blow his money on fancy cars or piss it against the wall like so many of his colleagues.

No, he would invest wisely, every penny he could—property, shares, precious metals. One day the world would surely go to hell, and he wanted to be sitting pretty looking down on the shitshow when it did.

It was getting dark when his Labrador, Mollie, came bounding in, reminding him it was time to take her for a walk. Deciding not to change and to take her on a short loop around the country lanes, he put her on a lead, and they headed out. Further down from his walled property, he had noticed car headlights but thought nothing of it. They went up around the lanes that skirted the woodlands nearby. Mollie pulled at the leash, eager to enter the woods as they usually would.

"Not tonight, Molly, sorry."

Joel's memory of what happened next was blurred. There was the wisp of movement in his peripheral vision, a moving shadow before someone grabbed him from behind and suffocated his face with a pungent sweet odour.

He heard the sound of glass breaking and then his senses faded to darkness.

Memory fragments.

In a vehicle. A low engine. Then coming round from his stifled coma. Another potent odour invaded his nostrils, followed by hard brutal slaps across his face.

"You will run," the voice said. "For your life."

And he had.

Now, trembling behind the tree, Joel knew he had to get going again to save himself. The thick woodland was all around him, waiting to swallow him up and shield him from the eyes of his pursuer.

Yet he couldn't. His body had frozen, muscles incapable of moving.

Get up. Get up and run. Now, Joel!

But he could not physically move.

He sensed the person first before hearing the slow, deliberate footfall approaching his position.

Please.

Joel began to whimper like a terrified child, his suit trousers slowly dampening as he urinated uncontrollably, and he wrapped his arms around his knees, waiting for death.

A rapid swish through the air.

Then a shockwave of pain exploded throughout his whole body. Joel collapsed, rolling on to his side with rapid gasps. With wide eyes, he looked down to see a metallic point protruding from his chest.

He coughed, and blood splattered over his once-crisp shirt. The light padding of footsteps drew closer before a boot pressed against his neck, shoving his face into the leaf-covered earth.

Joel heard his own scream bellow, the sound distant and detached, as the object was ripped out of him. A rough hand grabbed his hair, pulled his head back and rolled him over onto his back.

As consciousness was slipping, his vision blurred, Joel met the eyes of his killer.

He knew that face.

Joel tried to speak, to beg, but just coughed up thick dark blood, which sprayed from his mouth and into the air.

The figure held up a long object with a metallic point covered in blood that dripped onto the ground.

In one swift motion, it plunged into his throat. Joel's vision of the killer's face and the moonlit canopies behind ebbed away into darkness.

Chapter 2

It was the vast openness of the space that Douglas relished. The dawn sky overhead caught his attention and made him smile. It was the reason why he had driven here from their home in Bonar Bridge at six in the morning. A medley of fluffy clouds drifted idly against a pinkish hue. He breathed in the crisp, cold air.

He had driven along the narrow road as far as possible and parked up next to one of the low stone walls, then walked down towards the sea. He passed a derelict white stone cottage nestled into a rocky hill. Opposite, beyond a wooden fence, a rolling grassy hill turned to the stony beach. In front of him, the boat slipway, probably not used for a decade or more. For a moment, Douglas imagined what it might have been like there: the fishermen pushing the boat down the stone slope into the cold sea. It was hard not to picture it like some old black and white photograph from a time long since passed.

He stopped halfway along the slipway and breathed in the deep salty air.

Beautiful.

A gust of wind rippled his jacket and slacks, tussling his grey hair. He stepped off onto the fine beach stones and strolled on, gazing out across the North Sea.

He was so glad he had moved here. All his life had been knee-deep in the shitty and unforgiving world of criminality. He had spent most of his career either in Hong Kong or London, and in each city, in different ways, the dense metallic air had been painful to breathe. His memory wandered to Hong Kong and the last significant conflict of his career as a Detective Inspector, forced to cross swords with the psychopath rogue bomber, Richard Blyth, almost a year before.

Many lives had been lost, and he and his wife, Louise, had nearly lost theirs. After that, he was done with Hong Kong, and it didn't take much to persuade Louise to move back to the United Kingdom and the openness of the Scottish highlands.

A fresh and very remote start. It wasn't for everyone – the isolation needed absolute independence, which Douglas and Louise had enthusiastically dived into with the redevelopment of their two acres on the old farmhouse near Bonar Bridge. They now had a generously sized veg patch, a greenhouse, and a chicken hutch.

The new millennium beckoned and so did a new life, although a dark shadow loomed in Douglas's mind that caused him to grimace in the harsh wind.

He checked his watch. Louise would be waking up soon. Time to get back. Douglas had the sudden urge to get back home, to be with Louise. He always tried to have breakfast with her before the day started. There was work to be done in the garden. It was good to keep busy, he told himself over and over, to fend off the deep-seated worry inside. God knows what she must be going through.

He stopped walking and looked back to take it all in one last time. Beyond the slipway and rocky cliff, Douglas could see the tip of Tarbat Ness lighthouse.

Chapter 3

Douglas put down two bowls of porridge, poured them both coffee and sat down at the table.

"No eggs, I see?"

"Ah, no. I did look," Douglas replied before sipping his coffee.

Louise dripped maple syrup over her breakfast.

"How many days is that now?"

"A week, I think. Betty's laying days must be at an end. I'll ask Simon if he has another chicken or two." Simon was their local friend who had been the most hospitable of the locals, welcoming them to the area and helping them set up their little homestead.

"Maybe we'll be having a chicken dinner this Sunday?" Louise said, looking at him. He knew she wasn't joking. With her background growing up in Hong Kong, killing a chicken in the backyard was nothing unusual.

Douglas grimaced. "I got quite fond of the old bird."

Louise tutted. "Oh, don't be so sentimental."

Douglas gestured with his spoon to her bowl. "You like it?"

"Lovely as always, Doug. Maybe we should buy some eggs and things on the way back tomorrow?"

Douglas nodded, scooping up another mouthful of mushy porridge, then leaned back and stared out of the window that offered a panoramic view of the rolling hills. Dark clouds loomed, and he wondered if they would be able to work in the garden today at all.

"Appointment is 9.30?" he asked, solemnly.

"Yes, I'll check, but I'm sure it was."

They had called her in after the test results had returned. Couldn't be good. Douglas tried to remain stoic and cheerful, and Louise, being Louise, hadn't shown an ounce of worry or desire to talk about it. Just a simple, "Let's see what they say."

Any worry or concern had gone unspoken.

"Looks like any gardening is off today," Douglas said, peering once again over at the threatening sky.

"Well, I might read then. Let's see if it gets any better later on?"

Douglas grunted in agreement and began clearing away the dishes. Louise disappeared, and he settled into his favourite armchair before idly scanning through the newspaper. It was the usual sanitised crap they called news: the latest heatwave, or the cold snap. Celebs. Game shows gossip. The news contained less actual news every day, and Douglas wondered if journalists actually did any investigative work anymore.

A headline caught his eye: 'Man Found Speared in Banstead Wood Horror.' A photograph showed a policeman standing guard in woodland with tape behind him and the grim white-suited figures of forensics blurred in the background.

Douglas read on.

The body of Joel Hopkins, a Property conveyancer from Chessington, was discovered by a dog walker on Tuesday evening. The body had suffered multiple stab wounds with what police confirmed could have been a spear.

Many years ago, that had been his neck of the woods. Douglas wondered whether it wasn't outside the realms of possibility that, had he still been in his role as DI down in London, he would have been at the crime scene himself.

Douglas put down the newspaper and opened his laptop to check his email. His inbox was a mess, filled with junk mail that had still made it through his supposedly 'impregnable' spam filter. He started deleting the rubbish, his new morning routine that he hated but couldn't stop himself. It was like picking at a spot. You knew it was wrong, but you couldn't help yourself.

Doug spotted a familiar name amongst the crap. An email from Konrad Lynch, a Detective Superintendent from Douglas's Met days. He opened and read the email:

Doug! It's been a while I know. Hope you are keeping well? Would love to catch up in person. There is something I need to confer with you on too. Urgent. I can come up to your neck of the woods – it needs to be soon.

Konrad signed off with a number, asking for a phone call to make arrangements.

Douglas never forgot Konrad Lynch and never really liked him. It wasn't anything particular, just some characters didn't mix well, and Doug's quiet persona had grated with Konrad's brashness. He was a 'no-nonsense' DS, that was for sure.

Douglas re-read the email, stroking his chin. Reading between the lines, there was no doubt it was important. The question was what the hell would make him come up to Scotland from London?

***

Douglas walked into the hotel and scanned the plush lobby with polished marble floor and bronze awnings. Several guests were checking out in front of the dark wooden reception desk. Douglas spotted double doors to the bar and headed towards it.

He saw Konrad sitting by a Georgian window, eating a cooked breakfast and gave him a wave. Douglas was shocked by his appearance.

How long had it been? Fifteen, twenty years and the man had not aged well. Deep craggy face and a once bushy dark mane had been shaved short.

You're not precisely young yourself, Doug. Stop judging.

"How are you doing fella?" Konrad stood up, dabbing his mouth with a napkin and reaching out his hand. They were both similar in appearance; same height, their once muscular bodies, sagging now with age.

"Sorry, I couldn't wait. Absolutely starving," Konrad said, sitting down again.

Douglas waved his hand dismissively. "I ate already, no problem."

A young waitress approached and asked them if they needed anything.

"Just coffee, for me," Douglas replied.

"Yeah, I'll have another, thanks."

The waitress smiled and left.

"How is Louise?"

"Yes, she's good, good. She's here but wanted to look around the boutiques and market. We're not here much. I think she misses the bustle of Hong Kong."

"Great, that's great," said Konrad, absentmindedly.

"So how's life going in the big smoke?" Douglas asked.

Konrad pulled an expression of mock grimace.

"Like a steaming puddle of dog piss—always was, always will be."

Douglas chuckled.

"That description pretty much sums up why I left. Can't say I miss it."

Their coffees arrived, and they both took sips. When the waitress was out of earshot, Konrad leaned down and pulled out a folder from his bag.

"I wanted you to help me with something. Just take a look."

Douglas sighed, he thought this might be coming and whatever it was he knew he would decline. However, Konrad had come a long way.

He nodded. "Sure."

"Did you hear about the murder at Banstead Wood?"

"Yeah, a property chap wasn't he?"

Konrad nodded, his face neutral as he pushed the report across the table.

"Joel Hopkins. It appears he was grabbed while walking his dog, then ended in the woods. There were signs he had been chased or stalked for several hours before being killed. His dog was found nearby tied up to a tree."

Douglas opened it up and read some of the details from the toxicology report: the body temperature and degree of rigor mortis suggested death had taken place thirty six to sixty hours before police forensics had got to it. He looked over the photographs of the deceased; the body had been laid out deliberately. The hands were placed over the chest. Another picture displayed a symbol or sign drawn from little sticks pushed into the ground.

"What's this?" Douglas asked.

"No idea. A call sign?"

"Looks like tribal art, possibly African or something."

Douglas returned the photographs and report into the folder and pushed it back in Konrad's direction. "It sounds like an interesting case, but I don't see why—"

With a grim face, Konrad held up a photograph. The image of a male corpse on a concrete floor together with pools of dark blood. His face had been half caved in with some heavy weapon. Konrad, his face edging towards anger, held up another photo of the same man, alive, looking up with a broad smile from a restaurant table.

The face was familiar to Douglas, but he couldn't place it.

"My brother—Eric."

"Oh, Jesus."

Doug took the photos for a closer look.

"I'm sorry, Konrad—so sorry."

Konrad ignored the apology and jabbed a finger at the photo. "This was at his golf club. He was battered in the back of the head. A similar symbol laid out, that tribal shit. The same killer, Doug. Got my brother."

"What's the Met come up with?"

"Fuck all. That's the problem. We're spinning our tails, and there's very little to go on. We're dealing with someone smart and good at covering their tracks. You gotta help me catch this bastard, Douglas."

Just for a moment, Douglas sensed Konrad's desperation. He blew out air through his mouth.

"Look, forget my brother. It's not just about that—" Konrad added.

"I'm sorry about Eric. I really am. That's a shitty way to go, but I'm retired—I've got a life here. And how is the old firm going to think about me poking around?"

"You'd just be acting as a PI, working for me, fully and generously compensated, I'll get to the details if you're interested."

"Look, Douglas," Konrad said earnestly, "I know you're set on the quiet life but hear me out. There's a stipend, funded by some family and friends of both victims. It's very generous, and I'm hoping you will get to nail this psychopath."

Douglas gave out a light groan. The prospect of working again did in some small way intrigue him, but he had to think about Louise. She needed him right now, his support; this job would have him wrapped up in London for weeks.

"Look, Konrad. I've got something going on right now. Can't go into details but this isn't going to work. There must be someone else?"

Konrad cleared away the files and replaced them into his briefcase.

"I understand Douglas, I really do. In answer to your question: No, there's no one else. It's a delicate situation, and I need someone I can trust."

Douglas looked at his watch. "I need to go."

Konrad handed him a business card. "At least give it some more thought. My private number—in case things change."

Douglas pocketed it, shook hands with his old colleague and left the hotel.

Chapter 4

The small waiting room was sparse and smelt of disinfectant—just a row of blue plastic seats and a coffee table with magazines that were years old. Louise flipped through them anyway. Douglas felt a lack of oxygen, but the window was impossible to open, as if it was welded shut. There was a corkboard with various hospital leaflets and messages pinned up, spinning the bright side of life. After failing to open the window, Douglas paced a little, his eyes darting to the circular clock on the wall. They had been waiting for forty-five minutes for God's sake.

With that thought barely completed, the door opened, and a young female doctor peered inside.

"Louise Brown?"

They both looked over and nodded.

"I'm Mrs. Edmondson, the senior consultant. Come with me please."

They followed her down the hospital corridor then into a cupboard sized office. The consultant ushered them into seats then took her place behind the desk and opened a folder. She looked directly at Louise.

"Louise, thank you for coming by. So, as you can probably guess, the test results came back, and they are positive. I'm afraid you have early stages of bowel cancer."

Both Douglas and Louise stared back at her in shock. It was half expected, given the previous months of problems Louise had had health-wise but hearing the words felt like glass in the flesh.

"Oh God," Douglas muttered. He reached out for Louise, and they held each other's hands tightly.

"I know this is a lot to take on board; however, we have a programme of treatment that can begin immediately."

"What is the recovery rate of that?" Doug asked.

The consultant turned to her computer and clicked away at unseen files.

"I can tell you a woman of your age has over fifty per cent survival rate over five years. That's very good. Some only have five per cent or less."

She was sugar-coating, Douglas thought. It was fine, it was her job, and she probably had these conversations every single day. But to Douglas, that was a fifty per cent chance of dying too.

"Any other options?" Douglas asked with a wavering voice, edged with anger. He felt Louise squeeze his hand reassuringly then move it away.

The consultant clasped her hands together on the desk and smiled sympathetically. "There are drug treatments, of course. One, in particular, Bevacizumab, can help and has shown very promising results, pushing survival chances up into the near ninety per cent in some cases. Unfortunately, it's not yet available on the NHS and probably won't be for some time, in all honesty. And it's expensive."

"Oh?" Both Douglas and Louise looked at her, hopefully.

She opened a drawer and rummaged around before pulling out a leaflet, glanced at it briefly before pointedly handing it over to Louise.

"It targets and blocks a cancer cell protein called vascular endothelial growth factor and stops the cancer from growing blood vessels, starving it of oxygen so it cannot expand and grow," the consultant said, quickly.

Louise gazed over the text, looking confused, then handed it to Douglas who grabbed it and avidly scanned the details.

"Well that sounds better, right? It's what we need, huh, Lou?" He glanced over at her, encouraged, but she didn't seem to mirror his enthusiasm.

"We cannot afford it. It's expensive, Doug."

"Well, yes—" he trailed off, "maybe we can work something out." His mind raced for a solution. The money situation was dismal, and he felt growing anger that he had allowed it to get to this.

Douglas and Louise glanced at each other and stood up.

"I know this is a challenging time for you both, but we can manage this—the sooner, the better."

Douglas nodded. "Yes, thank you, Doctor."

***

The drive back was mostly silent apart from Douglas muttering that "we'll get through this" as he clutched the steering wheel. Louise was stoic, seemingly unaffected by the shocking news, but Douglas was well aware she was saving face. Inside, she would be devastated.

He had to find a way to pay for that private treatment, and his mind raced for a solution.

The move back to Scotland had been expensive. Their house was rented, and the landlord had insisted on six months rent in advance.

But that wasn't the real cause of their depleted wealth. Douglas had never been financially astute. His whole life had been a shitshow from that point of view. His early twenties and thirties had been a cesspit of alcoholism, gambling and credit card excess while he still somehow climbed the career ladder to DI. When he had got his life back on track and transferred to Hong Kong, the debt shadow never really went away. The problem had not been dealt with and buried.

Out of sight and all that.

Douglas thought about the curious case that Konrad had shoved in front of him. If he was serious about the compensation, if it was the real deal, then the answer was right in front of him. It was the last thing he wanted to do: go back into that world. He would have to leave Louise for long periods when she needed him most, but what choice did he have?

He pulled into the driveway of their detached cottage and switched off the engine.

"Louise. We need to have a shot at that private treatment. If the chances of success are that much higher, then we have to find a way."

Louise leaned her head back, her eyes closed. She looked remarkably young for fifty-five, more like late thirties, apart from the odd wrinkle and a few strands of grey in her jet black hair.

"We have nothing, Douglas. I have nothing."

"There is a way. That meeting I went to this morning. I was offered a job."

Louise shook her head, holding her fingertips on the bridge of her nose.

"No, Doug—you don't need to—"

"It's just an opportunity to do some PI work," he interrupted. "An investigation to help out an old friend. It'll pay for the private treatment you need, but unfortunately, I'll be away a lot, and I'm not sure how long it will go on for."

She turned to him, her eyes moist with tears.

"We're going to deal with this hon. We'll beat it, you and me. Let me do this for you."

They embraced for a few moments, and then both stepped out of the car. Louise unlocked the door, while Douglas turned and stared across the Kyle of Sutherland and the fields beyond. A grim expression of determination set on his face.

Chapter 5

The taxi pulled up outside a gated residence in East Molesey, a stone's throw from Hampton Court Palace. The high walls that surrounded the property suggested someone who liked their privacy.

Douglas paid the driver and hauled himself out of the back seat. As the taxi drove off, Douglas stared at the gated property grounds. From the road, the stone wall, bushes and trees hid whatever was beyond, but Douglas guessed it must be several steps up from his modest cottage in Bonar Bridge.

Not bad for an inspector's salary, Douglas thought.

He walked up to the entry comms panel and buzzed while peering through the gates. He could make out several cars parked on a gravel drive in front of an ivy-covered house, grand pillars standing either side of the front door. It looked like it was straight out of a Country Life magazine. He couldn't help feel a pang of jealousy. How life's path could be so different? They both had similar careers, and although Konrad had made Detective Superintendent it wasn't that much of a salary grade leap from his own.

Jealousy will get you nowhere, Douglas. Besides, under the circumstances, he's throwing you a much needed bone.

"Douglas! Welcome." Konrad's voice crackled through the intercom followed by a buzzing as the gates automatically slid open.

He walked through, up to the house and saw Konrad appear from the front door, giving him a wave. There was a distant bark of a dog from inside.

"Good to see you," Douglas said, approaching his old colleague. They shook hands and Konrad led Douglas inside.

"Hope the journey wasn't too arduous?"

"It was fine."

Douglas noticed the house looked bare, as if not lived in.

"Moving somewhere?"

"Ah, just a renovation. Long overdue."

They walked into the study where a young woman with long jet black hair and heavy eyeliner worked at a laptop.

"This is Sergeant Hazelle Miers. My assistant. She'll be working with you."

"Oh?" Douglas was surprised.

"Yes. She'll be helping you in an 'unofficial capacity' in her own time."

He looked at them both. "Right."

She stood up, smiled demurely and held out a pale hand which Douglas shook. She reminded Douglas of a goth teenager. Not what he was expecting.

"Good to meet you, Sergeant."

"Hazelle is fine," she replied.

Konrad opened a desk drawer and produced some paperwork and handed it to Douglas.

"Our agreement. Just to keep things clear. Providing you're happy, I'll get the first payment wired today."

Douglas exhaled with relief. The money Konrad was offering was more than generous, a day rate that put more than bread on the table. Plus he'd have all his expenses covered and a tidy bonus when he found the identity of the killer. He nodded his gratitude to Konrad before scanning through the contract. Then he took the Parker pen that Hazelle handed him and inhaled through his nose before signing it. If it wasn't for

Louise's cancer he wouldn't have gone anywhere near Konrad Lynch and his offer. His hideaway cottage in Scotland might have been modest but it was all he wanted.

"Good!" Konrad exclaimed as Douglas handed back the signed document. "Thank you for helping out, Douglas. I really appreciate it. Now, Hazelle will be able to assist with all the details of the cases so far. There will be an expenses account as mentioned in the contract for travel."

He handed Douglas a Visa card. "Just don't go wild, eh, Douglas?"

Douglas afforded a weak smile. "I'm planning on some heavy partying, Konrad. Don't you worry."

Konrad sniggered and slapped him on the shoulder. "Somehow I find that hard to imagine. You even shied away from a pint after work back in the day, I seem to remember."

"I always drink alone," he retorted.

Konrad smiled thinly, obviously unsure what that meant. He then handed Douglas an unopened letter. "This is a letter, signed by me for what it's worth, in case you have any trouble accessing crime scenes."

Douglas took it and slipped it into his inside jacket pocket.

"Hazelle has arranged a car you can use," Konrad added.

"Good, I forgot mine," Douglas quipped.

Konrad poured coffee from a cafetière and handed Douglas the cup.

"Hazelle will go through the cases so far with more detail—"

Douglas looked up at Konrad "—you're not sticking around?"

Konrad shook his head. "Afraid not, I'm absolutely snowed under, Douglas. Hazelle is well briefed and more than adequately qualified—"

Douglas looked apologetically at the young woman

"I didn't mean—"

"It's okay," she nodded curtly. "Whenever you're ready, Mr. Brown." She added with a hint of sarcasm.

Konrad held his hand out for Douglas.

"I'm sorry Douglas—urgent matters. You have my mobile. Let's catch up in a few days."

Konrad left, and Douglas took a look around the room, the dark wood paneling hosting a row of fine paintings, and sucked in air through his teeth. He began sifting through the file papers and focused on one page.

"Terrible to lose a brother like that," Douglas said.

Hazelle stood up and moved around the desk.

"Yes, absolutely. Found in the woods, near his golf club. Battered with his own club on the course."

Douglas nodded and flipped the page over to see a large print of the body of Eric Lynch lying prone on the ground. The same one Konrad had shown him.

"Yes, Konrad told me."

He picked up the other report and opened it up.

"Joel Hopkins, the most recent death, was found in Banstead Wood. Speared through the chest and throat," said Hazelle.

Douglas winced at the thought.

"So, both killed outside, in a similar way but with different murder weapons," continued Hazelle. "Then the bodies have all been moved after death with symbols left at each scene."

"Any clues to what they are?" Doug asked.

"Possible clan markings from East Africa, from what the semiotic expert says. But they seem unable to pin it down exactly."

"Alright. The crime scene for Eric's death sounds like a good first port of call. The golf club. Let's just drive over there and take a look."

"Yes, we shouldn't have any problems with access to any of these sites. Konrad has made sure of that. He can get us access to some of the reports. He is a DS after all." Hazelle was already putting on her camel coat.

Chapter 6

Douglas pulled into a parking space outside the elaborate white club-house at the Kingtree golf club, an exclusive haunt for a lot of well-moneyed types, according to Hazelle. The grounds were expansive, with the lush green course in every direction, interspersed with clumps of trees, woods and a small lake that sparkled in the sunshine. The course, Douglas noted, was empty of any players or carts.

"Looks like they still haven't re-opened the course—or it's a slow day."

As they got out of the hired Ford SUV, a young male concierge walked over to meet them.

"Mr. Brown?"

Seeing the confused look on Douglas's face, he continued, "Mr. Lynch called ahead and told us to expect you. Would you care for some refreshments before I show you to the scene?"

Douglas shook his head. "No, no, let's just get on with it."

They walked over to a waiting golf cart, and the concierge drove them across the immaculately kept course towards a small woods. There was police tape on the course, fencing off a patch.

"What's that?" asked Douglas.

"The place of suspected death. The body was moved to the wood," Hazelle replied.

They stopped at the edge of the woodland and got out. The concierge pointed them in the right direction and waited by the cart as Douglas and Hazelle headed into the tree line. Just a few metres in, under the breezy canopies overhead, they both spotted the police tape running around the tree trunks.

Hazelle opened her briefcase, took out and opened a folder, skimming through it to find the relevant information. "His body was found here," she gestured to the spot. Douglas slowly walked over, looking around the immediate area.

The symbols Douglas had already seen in the case photos were still laid out like a shrine. Small stones were arranged into a symbol like a sideways 'S' shape with points jutting outwards.

"Let me look at those images again," he said.

Hazelle rummaged through the file until she got them.

"Look at the way the body was positioned, definitely arranged into that pose on purpose," Hazelle, said, showing Douglas a photo.

Douglas hitched up his trousers slightly and kneeled onto his haunches to take a closer look.

"Know anything about tribal art, Hazelle?"

"Nothing other than what the report from the semiotics expert said. It is, as they say, a fucked up mystery."

"Let's look at the actual spot where he was killed."

They walked for several metres back on to the golf course and spotted the perfectly cut grass, streaked with blood.

"So, the body was dragged, but why go through all the effort?" Douglas said. "You're out here in the open, the deed's already done, and now you risk getting caught by moving the body. How far would you say it is, from where he died to where his body was found?"

"Sixty meters or so?" Hazelle said, glancing in front and behind herself.

"Do you know how much effort that would take? Clearly, the significance of the ritual at the end is of such importance that it's worth the risk."

They carried on walking towards the spot on the course.

"The reports say he was shot with an arrow through the right shoulder, fell to the ground, carried on crawling and then suffered a blunt force trauma to the back of the head," said Hazelle.

Douglas looked at the blotches of blood that had soaked into the grass, piecing together the final moments of the dying man.

"—that finished him off, no doubt," said Douglas.

"No doubt."

"And the murder weapon?"

"The Slazenger Iron was found over here. Belonged to Lynch and just had his prints over it. No one else's." She pointed to another taped spot a few metres away. The weapon, now long gone.

"What's the significance of moving the body do you think?" she asked.

"Well, by positioning the body, perhaps it's some final humiliating act? An act of dominance? But more than that, possibly, he wanted to take his time, not be disturbed. Talk me through what the police report says about the evening he was killed."

Hazelle quickly thumbed through the file again. "He played here regularly, most Thursdays, according to the club records. Last Thursday he was here, he played a full round with Greg Deason and Ron Blake. They finished their game at 19.30, returned to the clubhouse and spent a few hours in the bar. The CCTV shows him leaving the clubhouse at 21.45 as the clubhouse was closing, getting into his car and leaving the premises. His car was found the next morning at 06.15, parked in a layby, a few roads away by a passing motorist. There were no signs of damage to the car and no indications there was a struggle or fight within the car or near it—"

"So he leaves the clubhouse and heads, we presume, for home. He stops his car for some reason and then is abducted. No struggle would indicate he had his guard down; potentially knew his attacker. Our killer then brought him back to the course. Then, at some point, he is shot with an arrow and beaten over the head by the club. How far away was the car left?"

Hazelle thumbed through a few pages. "Approximately 700 metres in that direction," she said, pointing over her shoulder. "There are a few residential properties about, but if you knew which route to take you could avoid most of them."

Douglas followed the direction Hazelle was pointing. "Right, so we can speculate our killer possibly knew the victim, at least knew him well enough to be aware of his routine or had spent some time watching him. It's also likely this location was planned for the murder and the murderer knew the route he would have taken home and managed to get him out of his car without a struggle.

"Then Eric is brought here with no witnesses. Our victim then makes a run for it across the course, but his assailant catches up, manages to shoot him with a bow and then kills him with the club. Our killer drags the body across the course, spends some time positioning it. So what's our motive here?"

"Nothing obvious, no spouse to benefit from the inheritance. Apart from playing golf and working, it doesn't seem he did anything else."

"Have we got a list of everyone he regularly played golf with? Did the police file mark any potential suspects? Let's make a start and talk to them. I'm sure they won't mind going over it all a second time for us?" Douglas turned, his mind racing. He knew he was going to be going over exactly what the police had done; his only hope was that he found something they missed. "We might as well talk to security while we are here."

They headed back in the cart, driven by the concierge.

"We need to talk to someone about the security of the club?" Doug asked. "Any suggestions?"

The concierge turned his head. "That'll be Paul's department. I'll introduce you."

"Thanks."

He parked the cart and led them into the back door of the clubhouse and through a maze of corridors before the concierge stopped at a closed-door and knocked.

An old guy opened, a half-eaten cheese sandwich in one hand. Slowly munching, he looked from one of them to the other.

"This is PI Brown and his assistant. Wanted to ask you questions about security?"

"Right. Come in."

The concierge turned to Doug. "If you need me, I'll be at the clubhouse reception."

"Sure, thanks for your help."

Doug and Hazelle walked into the small windowless room. There was an old computer screen with a CCTV view of the clubhouse car park, a table with a toolbox on top and shelves filled with boxes.

Doug gestured with his head at the CCTV.

"I'm guessing nothing was caught on that?"

"Nope. Told the police that already." He munched the last of his sandwich, crumbs spilling on the floor.

"What areas does the CCTV cover?"

"Got a couple out front in the car park, one in reception, a couple in the bar and three that point out over the course."

"How far back do the recordings go?"

"We keep the last forty-five days on file. Then it just records over itself."

"Can we get a copy? Might be something obscure that was missed."

"You can, but as I said, nothing on there. I've looked, and the police have been through it as well."

"You're probably right, but it can't hurt to look."

Paul grunted, before sitting down. He took a blank disk and inserted it into a machine under the desk.

"Any break-in before at the club?"

"Nope."

"Is there any other vehicle access besides the main car park?"

"Nope."

Doug exchanged a glance with Hazelle and sighed.

"How long have you worked here? Paul?" Hazelle chimed in, struggling to hide the irritation.

"Forty—no forty-two years."

"What's the area like around here? You get much trouble from any of the locals?"

"Can't say we do."

"Not even the local kids up here messing around."

"Nope."

The machine beeped, Paul leaned down, took out the disk and handed it to Hazelle.

"Thank you." She mumbled, sliding the disk into her briefcase.

"Did you know the deceased?" Douglas continued.

"I've seen him around, can't say I've spoken to him though."

"I've seen enough here," Doug said. "Thank you for your time, Paul."

They left the room and headed for the car park.

"Let's check the Banstead Wood crime scene. We can get checked into a hotel near there and pay a visit first thing in the morning."

Chapter 7

Douglas picked up the phone off the desk. He pressed nine for an outside line and then dialled his home number and looked around the modest hotel room while the phone was ringing. They had found a hotel in Sutton, just fifteen minutes' drive from Banstead Wood. Deep red curtains hung down over the window through which he could see the lights of the local houses and offices—soft blue carpet underfoot and a bed that was far too big for one person.

"Louise?"

"Hi, Doug, how are you getting on?"

Douglas smiled. She still spoke with a hint of broken English, but it suddenly felt endearing to him. A wave of anxiety hit him, just for a moment, then he pushed his worries to the back of his mind.

He took a breath and turned the tumbler of Bourbon around in his fingers.

"Are you okay?" he asked.

She sighed, hesitated just for a moment, then said, "I'm fine. All is well. I miss you."

Douglas held one hand on his forehead as he spoke in a hushed whisper. "I miss you too. Listen, listen—there's great news. Some money is available so we can get that drug treatment the doc spoke about right away. We can get started—"

"Oh, Doug—that is great." He could hear the emotion at the back

27

of her throat, almost on the verge of breaking. She coughed, and they listened to each other breathing for a few seconds.

"So, call the consultant asap, okay honey?"

"Don't worry. I will."

"Great."

"And your case? Is it going okay?"

"Yeah, it feels like early days—very early days."

He had had this feeling before, and now he felt he was gravitating toward something terrible, something evil.

They spoke for an hour, then Douglas got ready for bed in the hotel, paid for by Konrad Lynch.

Chapter 8

Douglas looked up to the tree canopies and the perfect rays of sunlight streaming down to the uneven ground. Hazelle walked Douglas through the murder scene, along the trail where Joel Hopkins had run for his life.

"So what do we know?" Douglas asked, probing for a summary.

"Took his mutt for a walk—it would have been getting dark at that time. Our killer took Hopkins either by force or otherwise. Banstead Wood is about eight miles from his house in Chessington."

"It's a long walk that's for sure," Douglas agreed, "—but it's possible. How do you figure our killer took him to the woods?"

"Well, everyone that knows him said he takes his dog down Bluebell Lane and around the estate, almost like clockwork. It would have been very unusual for him to come out here."

They arrived at the oak tree. As the previous crime scene, police tape cordoned off an area around it. They soon saw the killer's signature: a series of small sticks that had been stuck into the ground creating another one of the mysterious symbols.

"The old calling card. What's our killer trying to tell us?"

After ten minutes of looking around and seeing nothing else unusual, Douglas buried his hands in his coat.

"There's some relatives of the victim we can speak to, that right?"

Hazelle nodded. "Yes, the wife and daughter."

***

Joel's wife, Helen, and their daughter, mid-twenties, both stood by the kitchen island using it as support. The daughter looked pissed off.

"We're just making sure nothing has been missed," Douglas soothed.

"We told the police everything we know, which is jack shit," the daughter said, with contempt.

"Laura!" Her mother wasn't impressed. She smiled apologetically at Douglas and Hazelle. "I'm sorry, this has been a distressing time, as you can—"

"You should check out Robert Harrington. He got nasty with Daddy, a big land deal—it was in the local news."

The mother shot her a stern look but said nothing.

"No, I'm going to say it. Robert Harrington harassed my father. I remember overhearing a call once when they were shouting at each other. He's someone you should question—"

"You didn't mention this to the police?"

"What's the point—oh look, just forget I said it," Laura said with contempt. She strutted to the sink and poured herself a glass of water.

It didn't seem relevant, but Douglas took out his notepad. "If you don't mind—I'd like to take any names of interest," Douglas said. "Where can I find this—Robert Harrington?"

"He sometimes drinks at the Mozart's club in Chertsey. That's all I know," Helen said.

"Was there anyone else you can think of that might have wanted to hurt your husband?"

"No, I'm sorry. My husband was a shrewd businessman, sure he stepped on a few toes now and then but that's business, right?"

"Does the name Eric Lynch mean anything to you?"

"I can't say that it does. My husband did business with a lot of people. You should check with his office, though. They'll keep records of his appointments."

"Ok, well, thanks for your time. If there is anything else you think of, here is my mobile number."

Chapter 9

The killer had parked on the driveway of one of the half-built houses on the sprawling housing development in Ealing, West London, just out of sight. It was five to seven in the morning on a Sunday, and there would be no work crews coming on site today.

He watched the cul-de-sac where the four near-completed houses stood. Scattered around the site, diggers, cranes and other machinery lay dormant, frozen like statues.

A black Mercedes turned into the site, past the row of Portakabins near the entrance and moved slowly down the dusty hill road. It stopped for a few moments, the driver unsure of their destination, before speeding up with a screech and pulling around alongside the cul-de-sac.

The financial trader, William Leung, got out and looked around, clearly annoyed at having to be here so early. He wore jeans and an expensive puffy jacket. He walked up to the doorway of the first house and peeped inside.

The killer opened his door and sauntered towards him, casually as if strolling down a high street, window shopping. As he got to the Mercedes, Leung turned and saw him.

"Ah, there you are! This is a fucking joke, meeting here at this time. You dare blackmail me?" Then he hesitated, a frown appearing. "Do I know you?"

The killer smiled to himself. It was always the way, the rhetoric of arrogant and privileged men. Instead of replying, he opened his jacket and drew out a large hunting knife.

Leung paled. "What are you doing with that?"

He looked around frantically. The killer was between him and his car, and the pile of brick pallets blocked any quick escape across the building site. He took a step back into the house, almost stumbling over the doorstep but grabbed the edge of the doorway and righted himself.

"Who the fuck are you? Is this about—? Listen, we can work this out. Do you need money? I have plenty—" Somehow, he realised his assailant wasn't listening or caring and stopped babbling. Then he held his hands around his mouth and screamed: "Heeeeeelp me!"

The killer took a few sudden steps towards him, and Leung turned on his heel and ran inside the building. He moved quickly, following Leung into what would be the front room, knowing there was only one way to run. It had not taken much to set up, a window or door blocked here or there and the small maze had been created.

He strode on, through the funnelled route his victim had to take. There was a desperate sound of a door being rattled violently, and then the footfall moved on, accompanied by the crash of buckets and falling work tools.

Footsteps hurried into the large kitchen space before a whooshing creak, followed by a resounding thud, boomed through the house. The ground shook.

A low guttural cry.

The killer stepped into the space, knife in hand and looked down at Leung's twitching body. Even better than he had planned, the steel beam had fallen directly onto his body, trapping him on the ground.

He pressed his boot onto an outstretched arm and leaned down close, wanting his face to be the last thing that Leung would see. But the banker's eyes were flickering and rolling around in his head, the last remnants of life.

A whimpering escaped his mouth, then the sound of deep gargling from within his chest.

"Pity," the killer muttered, rolling his fingers over his blade.

Chapter 10

The meeting had been set by Hazelle back at the golf club with two friends of Eric's. Two older men, clearly golfers from their white slacks and powder coloured sweaters, were sitting at a corner table, having a quiet conversation over a couple of gins. They stopped talking as Douglas and Hazelle approached.

"Still waiting for the course to open, gents?" asked Douglas.

"We'd come here anyway, get away from the wives," one of the men with cropped grey hair said with a smirk. "We already spoke to the cops, but if it helps find Eric's murderer, we're happy to tell you what we told them."

"Thanks. I appreciate that," Doug replied, taking a seat. Hazelle pulled up a chair alongside.

The other golfer, an obese man with a thin moustache, drained his G and T.

"So, Mr. Ron Blake, Greg Deason. How well did you know Eric?"

"We played a few rounds when we could. He was a busy man, we all are," said Blake, who put down his glass.

"Know anyone who might want to do him harm?" Doug asked.

"Someone who might want to club him to death?" Hazelle interjected. Doug gave her a disapproving look.

Both golfers, in turn, glanced at each other.

"Well, there was something. We don't know for sure, but we always thought Eric might be involved in that property deal," Blake said, quietly. "Some complained it was a scam, so I heard. There were a few disgruntled investors. Well, Eric was involved in that Oak Tree Holdings."

"Yes," the other golfer said, chiming in, "he may have taken the blame?"

"Was Eric seeing anyone, a girlfriend or partner that he spoke about?"

"He was always talking about women that he'd been with, this girl or that. The man didn't seem like he was the settling down type. You think this could have been the act of a jealous lover?"

"Right now, we are looking into every possibility. Can you remember any of the names of the women?"

Both men chuckled. "Possibly a first name but not much more than that."

"Do you know Joel Hopkins?"

Both men shook their heads dismissively. "Not a name that I remember, although it's getting harder to recall things these days."

Doug thanked the men, then he and Hazelle headed for the exit.

"Would that be enough motive? To be a victim of a multi-million-pound scam?" Hazelle asked as they headed to the car.

"Let's see what we find." Doug was smiling for the first time in days.

He felt a buzzing in his coat pocket and fished out his Nokia. It was Konrad.

"There's been another one," he said, the fear laced in his voice.

Chapter 11

Calston Mews housing development in Ealing was a sprawl of new-build houses that were in various stages of completion with gaps for the waiting windows and exposed roof beams.

They drove to the edge of the estate and parked alongside several police cars. Hazelle flashed her warrant card and spoke to the constable on watch briefly before they were ushered through into the sprawling building site.

They approached a cul-de-sac of four houses, taped off, and a couple of suited figures walked up towards them. One, a tall Afro-Caribbean man, grew more familiar to Douglas as he approached.

Was that DS Milner?

His colleague was a shorter man Douglas didn't know—a stocky type in jeans and a bomber jacket.

"I thought that was you. Come out of retirement, Douglas Brown?" Milner said, with a heavy hint of sarcasm.

"Just helping an old friend piece this shitshow together. How are you, Detective Sergeant?"

Milner assessed Douglas for a moment and glanced over at Hazelle who didn't offer any greeting.

"You realise this is an ongoing investigation, Doug?" Milner said.

"Forgive me mate, but I'm not even sure—"

Douglas exhaled impatiently. "DS Konrad Lynch has got me on the runaround. He's pissed right off."

"Oh?" Milner looked concerned. Seemed Konrad had influence.

"He doesn't think the investigation is going anywhere," Douglas replied casually.

Milner glanced at his mate. "It's going fine," he retorted.

"Can't spare me the lowdown then?" Douglas asked.

Milner looked uncertain and stuffed his hands into his trouser pockets, but there was no cold chill in the air.

"Well, we're done here I suppose. For now. Site manager found the body yesterday morning at the back door of the end house there." Milner jerked his head to one of the houses. "Blunt force trauma, by an RSJ beam."

Milner leaned towards Douglas, lowering his head slightly. "Weird thing is there were some alterations on-site. Doors blocked, one of the hallways blocked and a beam moved into a position that killed Leung. All very strange. You'll see it."

Milner gestured to his colleague with a jerk of the head. "Gotta go. Nice seeing you, Douglas. Say goodbye to your girlfriend." He winked at Hazelle who glared back.

Douglas and Hazelle continued walking to the houses, stepping inside the last house and walking through the interior. At the end of the building, which Douglas guessed was going to be a kitchen one day, a large blood patch was soaked into the ground. The same tribal markings as the others.

"Another one running away from his pursuer?" asked Hazelle.

"Looks like it," replied Douglas.

They began slowly walking through the house following a trail of police markings: a wheelbarrow knocked over on its side, scuff marks on the ground where the victim fell while running, hand marks on doors that were blocked.

They retraced their steps back outside. Hazelle pointed to the cul-de-sac road. "This is where his Merc was found.".

"So he drove here. To meet someone? Either very late at night or early morning."

Douglas walked into the road and turned back to face the houses.

"Looking at it from this angle, if he was near the door and was approached by his pursuer, the only option was to run into the house. Then he's like a rat in a maze, nowhere to go except towards the door at the back.

"I doubt this was a scheduled meeting of any kind," Douglas surmised. "So we can assume Leung was contacted by the killer to meet him here. Who could do that? Call our victim and get them here and on what grounds? Would he have come down if he felt threatened at all?"

"Blackmail maybe? Something he wanted to keep quiet and settle privately?" Hazelle suggested.

"A possibility. Or someone he knew, perhaps got a call or message from a friend, someone who needed help? So what info have we got on the victim? This William Leung?"

"Report's in my case in the car." Hazelle gestured to the vehicle.

"Alright. Let's go."

Inside the car, Hazelle fished out Leung's details and began to read out the details.

"So William Leung from Richmond. Originally from Singapore. Married for fifteen years but his wife went back to Asia. No previous offences. A financial trader but also, and yes, get this—a director with Oak Castle Holdings."

"Right. That's another connection with this Robert Harrington. Think we need to eyeball him, see where he was on the dates of the murders."

Chapter 12

After the drive back to the hotel in Sutton, Douglas showered, changed into the hotel-branded dressing gown and took his evening meal through room service: Steamed salmon and vegetables with mineral water. He fought the urge to counteract the healthy dinner with a Bourbon and a scrouged cigarette. He felt exhausted, washed out and looked forward to an early night. The months of idyllic life had not prepared him for a return to the old game very well.

After eating, he opened his laptop and went in search of this property deal involving Oak Castle Holdings.

Doug opened Google and began searching.

He soon found a news article which claimed a couple of investors, including Robert Harrington, had indeed alleged they were victims of a scam. They bought into a land deal, a lucrative opportunity to get in on the ground floor for a new major development. The plans outlined designs for a small community sat on the outskirts of London. Good facilities and good transport connections.

However, all assured planning permission never got granted, and what the investors paid for the land was well above what they should have for land without the permission to build.

Instead of potentially making hundreds of millions, the investors claimed they had been duped for a substantial amount. The story gave no other details and claimed the investigation was ongoing but speculated it would soon be closed due to lack of evidence.

Could being duped out of heaven knows how much money be a motive to brutally kill?

Harrington had lost a lot of money, along with others—perhaps an unhinged mind had snapped at the seams? It would at least be worth eyeballing him, Douglas thought.

He picked up the bedside phone and dialled Hazelle's room number. She answered after a few rings. "Hello."

"Thought you'd be out partying?"

"Ah, well I was just heading out."

"Really?"

She tutted. "No. Nothing much happening in Sutton."

"Listen, can we go over and see this Robert Harrington first thing? I want to get a handle on this Oak Castle set up."

"Sure, when do you want to leave?"

"Let's get breakfast as soon as they serve it and be on the road for seven."

"Right."

"Don't like early starts, Hazelle?"

"I love them," she said flatly.

"Great, see you in the restaurant at six."

The line cut off without another word and Douglas put down the receiver with a wry smile.

Standing up and stretching, Douglas walked over to his pile of clothes, heaped on the back of a chair. He rummaged through the pockets, pulling out the disk with CCTV footage from the golf course, then slid the disk into his computer and started scanning through the footage. About fifteen minutes into watching the footage on fast forward, he called room service and ordered a double Bourbon.

If it's another long night, might as well make the most of it—

41

Chapter 13

The killer checked his watch. It was almost lunchtime. He could hear another round of shotguns sporadically firing, taking out any unlucky pheasant that came within range.

It was time. He opened up the email app and found the draft he had written earlier and hit send. Then he made the call to Amerate Gonji's wife. When she answered, the killer spoke in the most distinct voice he could muster.

"Mrs. Gonji, my name is Max. I am a private investigator, hired by a gentleman called Mr. Kingston to investigate whether his wife was having an affair."

"What? I'm sorry, what has this to do with me?" she asked, confusion and doubt edging into her voice.

"My investigation led me to find out that Mrs. Kingston was having an affair. When I showed the evidence to Mr. Kingston, he asked about the man she was sleeping with and insisted that if he was a married man that I was to do the right thing and tell his wife." He paused before continuing. "That, unfortunately, is the reason for my call."

"I don't—"

"I know this is hard to take in, but as instructed by Mr Kingston, I have forwarded you in an email all the evidence I have collected. My contact details are on the email if you should have any further questions. Again, I'm sorry to call you out of the blue and be the bearer of bad news."

With that, he hung up and switched the phone off.

He took out his monocular; from his viewpoint, he could make out a group of hunters. It was lunchtime, and they were starting to head back to the road where several 4x4 vehicles waited to take them back to the lodge.

He surveyed the men, laughing and joking, and scanned for his intended target. Gonji was a big man and the only man of African descent amongst the killer's victims. How he had become part of this white man's group, the killer had no idea, but he would die just the same.

He watched as they strolled through the valley. And then his victim's phone rang. Although he couldn't hear what was being said, he could see the change in the body language. The posture-breaking, shoulders slumping, the realisation his little secret was out.

Gonji waved his waiting friends away, who continued. Then he started to become more animated, waving his hands, no doubt trying to defend his actions.

The killer looked up, all but one of the 4x4s had gone now, left for lunch. Slowly he got up, making his way down the hillside towards his victim. Walking cautiously, he kept himself small and hidden. Not that there was much point with Gonji so engrossed in his conversation.

He waited just out of sight behind a bush, around fifty metres away. His victim was pacing up and down, his shotgun placed against a low stone wall.

When Gonji's back was turned, the killer stepped out. Walking purposely towards him, as the killer didn't want his victim running too soon. Part of this was the thrill of the chase, after all.

He closed the ground quickly when he was ten metres away. His victim was still none the wiser.

"Gonji!"

Gonji turned and stared. Instant recognition.

Gonji's eyes darted towards his shotgun, resting on the low wall; it was in between them now. The killer could see him weighing up his options. Then he turned and took off in a dead sprint up the track. His phone dropped into the long grass. Surprisingly fast for a big man, thought the killer, who grabbed the shotgun and checked the barrel.

Good. Fully loaded.

Gonji was fast, but the killer could easily match his speed. The sharp incline out of the valley soon had Gonji slowing, drawing in deep breaths and struggling to maintain the pace.

He raised the rifle and set his sights on the fleeing Gonji, slowly pressing the trigger. The shot rang out, and the big man stumbled and fell.

Winged like a bird.

The killer took off at a steady jog to reach his prey.

There was a cry, a shout for help, but no one could hear him. His hunting friends were long gone.

When the killer caught sight of Gonji again, the man was on his knees in long grass, struggling to get onto his feet, his right hand clutched a bloodied arm. He turned, sweaty faced and looked in terror at his pursuer.

"Please," he shouted, "stop this!"

His hunter raised the rifle once again and fired. The burst of blood and brains splattered over the green foliage and Gonji's body fell flat into the soft mud.

Chapter 14

The following morning, torrential rain pelted the windscreen as Douglas and Hazelle headed to Ottershaw, north of Woking.

"So what's your thinking on this property deal?" Hazelle asked, chewing on a pastry she had grabbed from the breakfast buffet. She had been late and took a coffee and pastry to go. Douglas took the wheel.

"Not really sure yet. It'll be good to unpeel a few layers on this property deal. Our victims were all part of it. All had some interest in Oak Castle Holdings."

"Let's see what Mr. Harrington has to say," Hazelle chimed in between mouthfuls of croissant.

An hour later, they pulled up alongside a multi-storey Georgian building that had been converted into offices. There was an archway next to it that led into some courtyard. The rain had eased off, but there were still people huddled under umbrellas, hurrying along the street against a vicious wind.

Douglas glanced at his watch.

"Good timing. He should be here anytime now."

They waited for twenty minutes until a Jaguar reverse parked just a few metres ahead of them.

"This him?"

The bearded figure in a dark suit got out of the car, leaned back in and pulled out a laptop bag.

Hazelle consulted her report paper.

"Matches his description."

"Alright, let's go."

Douglas leapt into action and half jogged after the man as he approached the building. He timed it as Harrington was opening the front door.

"Mr. Harrington!"

He looked around with an anxious look of surprise.

"Yes?"

"Douglas Brown. I'm a private investigator working with some families of recent murder victims. Do you have five minutes?"

Hazelle walked up alongside Douglas.

"This is Hazelle Miers, who is assisting me."

Harrington looked at them both with suspicion.

"I already talked to the police."

"Well, the police are looking at your part in all this," he lied. "I want to clear some things up. It'll be quick."

Harrington reluctantly gestured them inside.

In his spacious office, they took a seat around a coffee table.

"So you were an investor with the Oak Castle Housing Project?"

"Yes, that's right."

"And you lost a substantial amount of money?"

Harrington's face seemed to darken at the memory.

"An understatement—"

"How, exactly? Can you talk me through it?"

"Well, we were misled as investors. Made to believe the land had the correct permissions for building, and it didn't. It looked perfect—around thirty houses, retail outlets and great links to the motorway. I was conned, well and truly. It could have been a substantial profit; instead, I'm stuck with a green belt that I cannot build on at all—not to mention they got away with it."

"And Joel Hopkins, Eric Lynch and Will Leung are all behind this Oak Castle Holdings Group?"

"Yes, that is right."

"Did you know they are all dead, Mr. Harrington?"

Harrington stared at Douglas, who observed his reaction.

"I knew that Hopkins and Lynch were but not Leung."

He looked suitably shocked, but Douglas wasn't sure.

"Where were you on the 12th of October, between 5-11 pm?"

It was the date and time of Eric Lynch's death.

"I'd have to check my calendar, but I can assure you I had nothing to do with his or any of those other deaths." He laughed, dismissively, then leaned over, pulled a MacBook out of his bag and fired it up.

"Well, while you're at it, can you check these other dates and times too?" Douglas read out the estimated times of deaths for Joel Hopkins and Will Leung.

Harrington shot Douglas an offended look, sighed with irritation and focused on his screen.

"Ah yes, well, I was at Mozart's on the 12th."

"Mozart's, is that the posh place on London street?"

"Yes, it's a members club."

"How did you get there? Not drinking and driving, surely? And you can't walk from where you live."

Harrington cleared his throat. "No, I called a cab."

"The company?"

"I—don't remember."

Douglas watched his face, the way the lines contorted and the movement of his eyes. He was lying, Douglas was sure of it.

"Beezer cabs."

Douglas looked at Hazelle, who got her phone out and walked away.

"What about the 16th of October? It was a Sunday. Your movements on that day?" Douglas had the death of Will Leung at the building site in

47

mind.

"Er—well, I'm not sure of that either. Bowling, perhaps. No, I was at home, alone."

Douglas studied him closely.

Hazelle returned, holding up her phone.

"No such booking at Beezer Taxis."

"You're lying, Mr. Harrington. What are you hiding?"

"Look, I did not murder those men, much as I would've liked to. I was in a card game. Gambling. I didn't want my wife to know. My debts are mounting, and I've been an idiot, trying to gain some more cash to smooth things over." Harrington was looking sorrowful now.

"Can you prove that?"

"Should I have to? Look, I came clean with the police. Told them everything; they checked it out and gave me the all-clear. The bad deal has put a strain on my marriage. If she finds out about this, then we'd be over."

Douglas heard the chirping of his phone.

"Excuse me. I need to take this." He took out his phone and saw it was Konrad Lynch.

Douglas barely got a greeting in before Konrad started babbling.

"There's been another one. In Wales. A fucking shotgun, and yes it's our same killer. This is getting serious now, Doug. You need to get a grip and make some progress on this investigation."

Douglas looked at Hazelle and Harrington who were both looking at him, intrigued. He held up his hand, signalling them to give him a moment, then left the office and stood in the corridor.

"When did this murder happen?" Douglas whispered.

"I don't know exactly when, but it happened in the last few hours."

"Shit!"

"What?"

"That time scale puts our main suspect in the clear." Douglas's shoulders slumped, almost feeling the weight of the case starting to bring him down.

"You'd better get back to the drawing board, Doug. Our killer seems to be just getting started."

Chapter 15

"Another rich person's paradise," Douglas muttered as he looked down into the approaching valley and their destination, a red brick, aged manor house surrounded by vast swathes of manicured gardens and stables.

It was almost impossible not to feel a hint of jealousy.

Rich people with their vast properties and land. Deserved through hard work and smart thinking, no doubt. But most would be inherited wealth, retained and kept close to the chests of the elites. It was always the 99 per cent who lost out.

He would have given that thought a lot more attention except he was trying to piece the cobwebs of the investigation together in his mind. The property angle had seemed like it had been a possible motive, until now. What connected all the victims, apart from the symbols left at each of the scenes?

"What have we got on this victim?" Douglas asked.

"Amaete Gonji, a Zimbabwean national who went to Eton. He was a director with Oak Castle Holdings and his father was part of the government in Zimbabwe."

"Hmmm. Let's not discount a hired killer. Maybe Harrington or one of the other scam victims got someone to do their dirty work."

"But Harrington? Does he seem likely to have?"

"What do you think? We need to deal in cold facts, but who bloody knows in this day and age?" Douglas muttered.

At the gates, several police officers gestured at them to stop. Hazelle lowered her window and held up her warrant card.

"Douglas Brown and Hazelle Miers. We're here at the behest of Detective Superintendent Konrad Lynch." Hazelle spoke for them both, with authority that made Douglas smile.

They were waved through and drove into a pebbled driveway and parked up alongside rows of police vehicles and civvy Land Rovers. The crime scene was teeming with officers coming to and from the house.

Douglas recognised DS Milner. That meant this murder was being treated as if connected to the others. Otherwise, it would just be the local police involved.

They stepped out of the car and Douglas immediately spotted a man in a tweed suit smoking a cigarette, leaning against a stone garden wall.

"Would love one of those," Douglas said, cheerfully.

The man looked up. Baby faced. Pampered. He offered his pack of cigarettes, but Douglas held up a hand.

"Gave it up a long time."

The man snorted with derision.

"I already gave my statement."

"I know—I understand, and going over it all again—bloody annoying, but if you could, it would help—a lot."

The man crushed his cigarette butt under his boot.

"Go ahead then, if you must."

"Your name?"

"John Smyth."

"And you knew the victim?"

"Not that well."

"So explain what happened. From the beginning."

"We were out hunting pheasant, six of us. On the pegs from around 9:30 am. The morning drives had been good."

"Sorry, what is that? The pegs? The drives?"

"The pegs just mean the position or location the hunters take when hunting. The 'drives' are when the beaters make a noise to scare the birds into flight. Does that make sense, old man?"

"Carry on."

"We were returning to the lodge for lunch when Amaete's phone rang. The call seemed important, so we left him to it and walked on, taking our Rovers back to the main house for lunch. When he didn't return at all, we became a little concerned. I called his phone, but it went straight to voicemail. I assumed he was still on the call. It's not unusual for problems at work to take a while to resolve. As we finished lunch and got ready to return to the pegs, he still hadn't responded. When we couldn't find him in the lodge, we figured he must still be out in the valley."

Smyth checked his Rolex watch and looked up at Douglas with a bored expression.

"Then what?"

"We drove back out, and his 4x4 was where he had left it, but Amaete was nowhere to be seen. We spread out to do a quick search of the area. It's pretty rough terrain out there, and we guessed that he must have taken a fall. It was Jeffery who found the body, about 100 metres up in a wooded area from where the pegs were."

"Do you know anyone who might have wanted him dead?"

Smyth shook his head. "No."

"What did he do for a career?"

"He was in property development as far as I knew. We don't discuss business on our shoots."

Douglas doubted that but let it slide.

"Thanks for your help, Mr. Smyth."

Douglas turned to Hazelle.

"Think we should go look at the scene if we can."

Hazelle spoke to another policeman then gestured to Douglas to head to the car.

"It's a bit of a drive to the crime scene."

They got back into the car and headed back onto the road and continued down a hill, then pulled into a side road that led to a space on the edge of a woodland that also looked like a car park with numerous police vehicles. They parked and approached the forensic scene investigator (FSI).

"We'd like to see the crime scene," Douglas said.

"No one outside the investigation unit is permitted," the officer replied, staring at Hazelle's warrant card. Douglas, in turn, read his name badge: Dean Adams.

Douglas reached into his inside jacket pocket and pulled out the signed letter Konrad had given him. Adam read it and nodded.

"Alright. You'll need to suit up. PPE in the van," Adams said, pointing to a white vehicle.

"Naturally," Douglas replied.

Once the white PPE suits were on over their clothes, Douglas and Hazelle, escorted by the FSI, made their way along a mud track marked by orange cones before coming to the pegs.

There were forensic photographers taking pictures of everything in sight. A series of numbered cones marked spots of interest. Further away, through a thicket of bushes, a small white tent had been erected over the body.

Douglas gestured at one of the cones.

"What was there?"

"The victim's mobile phone," Adams replied.

Douglas nodded.

"So this is where he started to run; something spooked him?" Hazelle was looking around as if a clue lay in the trees.

"You're out here carrying a shotgun, your phone rings, an important call. What would he do with his gun? What would you do? You'd put it down, answer the call."

Douglas looked around and immediately spotted a low stone wall, covered in ivy.

"Placed here perhaps." Douglas gestured at the wall. "Maybe he paced around while on the phone. Agitated."

Douglas began pacing himself as if mimicking Amaete's past movements.

"And then he ran down the track in that direction. So our killer approached him from over there." He indicated with a nod of the head.

They approached the tent along the track, and Douglas looked down at the body of Amaete Gonji. He was slumped on his front, face down, torso half twisted. There was a gaping shot wound in the back of his head and another in his arm, having ripped through his barber jacket. There was an unusual marking drawn on the back of his barber jacket in chalk—a vertical squiggle with what looked like blades jutting out from the top and the bottom.

"Shot while running?" Hazelle commented.

"With that marking again."

Douglas turned to Adams. "I take it there's a record of his phone calls?"

"Two calls. One unknown: a 'Pay as you Go' sim card was used. Then, his wife. He had an affair, and she had received the proof," said Adams. "Not a happy bunny I imagine," he added.

"She received proof? From who?"

"A throwaway Yahoo! email address. But that's gone nowhere. Hard to trace."

"Hmmm." Doug stared down at the body. The symbol. Was he leaving a clue deliberately? Was he targeting them because of their wealth?

Adams shook his head and glanced at his watch.

"Ok, I'm out of here. I'm afraid you'll have to leave now."

CHAPTER 15

Chapter 16

"Let's have a break. Can you stop at the next services?" Douglas asked.

"Sure. Hankering for a Maccy D?"

"God, no." Douglas almost snorted with derision. He could tell Hazelle was trying to lighten things up a bit. Ever since the Manor House in Wales, he had said very little, answering her with mere grunts.

With Harrington he thought he had got a scent; it had seemed likely he was a potential suspect, but now that had to be dismissed.

They pulled into the car park.

"I'm just going to the toilets. Meet you at Starbucks?"

After visiting the men's room, Douglas loitered by a newsagent, took out his phone and rang Louise.

"Hey Lou."

"Douglas. How are you?" She sounded weak.

"Fine, fine. Don't worry about me, hon. How is the treatment?"

"Well, the first round is nearly finished. It has helped the pain, yes."

"Great."

"The first batch of pills are nearly finished though, so are they sending more?"

"Yes, I'll find out."

It meant further large payments. He'd need to speak to Konrad.

"Is your work going ok?" she asked.

"Well, a few potholes in the road—"

"Oh."

"I'll get onto this now then."

"Speak soon."

Douglas disconnected and rang Konrad, who answered quickly.

"You find something?" he asked breathlessly.

"Erm, no. I just wanted some clarification on the payments. I need some more."

"I'm sorry Douglas, the contract stipulates payments based on progress in the case. You need to track this person down."

"What?"

"You need to nail this, Douglas."

"Well, I bloody well know that, Konrad. I'm on it. What I didn't realise is there would be a problem getting paid!"

"Read the contract, Douglas. I've paid one instalment to get you started—you spent it already? I want to progress—then you get more coin."

Douglas gritted his teeth. He didn't want to say anything about Louise, her cancer—but what choice did he have?

"Listen, Konrad," Douglas's tone was calmer. "Louise is seriously ill. I need to pay for some costly treatment—"

There was a pause and a sigh.

"Look. I'm sorry to hear that, but it's not just about me holding back money. I've had to re-organise things, sell assets—it takes time."

Bullshit.

Douglas didn't believe that for a second, but he bit his lip.

"Get results, Douglas—I'll see what I can do."

The line clicked dead.

Douglas slid the phone back into his pocket. What would he tell Louise now? He wanted to shout, punch the wall and let out his anger. Instead, he took a deep breath, composed himself and headed to Starbucks.

He sat down next to Hazelle, and she slid over a coffee.

"Thanks," he half mumbled, his mind still thinking of Louise. "What's our next move then?"

Douglas sighed, straightened himself up in the chair and pushed thoughts of Louise out of his mind. If he was going to help her, he needed to get his game on.

"So far, the only connection we have found is Oak Castle Holdings and the alleged scam. We can ask the police to pull the financial records to see, even if Mr. Harrington didn't commit the murders, did he pay someone else to do so? From his current financial situation it's unlikely, but let's chase it down anyway. The fact all the victims were on the board of the same company eluded that they all knew each other through work and probably outside of work. Let's take a closer look, dig deeper into their social lives and see what we can find out."

"Where shall we start then?"

"Let's head to Eric Lynch's house. He had no wife and kids to get in our way. See if there's anything that can shed light on this. Where was his house?"

Hazelle checked her notepad. "Weybridge. What are we looking for?"

"We probably won't know until we see it."

Chapter 17

It was a good three-hour drive back towards London. Just before Weybridge, they turned into a secluded country road that led to a private residence. Douglas opened a gate, and they drove through into an oblong, gravelled courtyard with stables on either side. Set back behind them was a country house. There was one car parked: a Mini Cooper.

After several minutes of knocking, there were finally signs of life and a woman in her fifties answered—the housekeeper.

"Good afternoon. I'm Douglas Brown, a private investigator, and this is Hazelle Miers." Hazelle held up her identity card that seemed to impress the woman. "We have been hired by Konrad Lynch to investigate Eric Lynch's death. Do you think we can look around the house?"

The woman nodded compliantly and let them in.

"A terrible business," she muttered. "Have they caught the killers yet?"

"Not yet." Douglas gestured to the first ground floor rooms. "So, do you mind?"

"Go ahead. Do you want tea or coffee?"

"I'm good, thank you." Hazelle shook her head. "No, thanks."

Douglas turned to Hazelle as the housekeeper disappeared.

"We'll split up. You start upstairs."

"Right."

Douglas walked into the dining room to a chiming grandfather clock.

Two sash windows adorned with dark red curtains offered views of a picturesque garden. He beelined to a writing table and opened the drawers. A Parker pen and a notepad neatly positioned inside. After a few minutes, he moved across the hallway into another living room: puffy sofas, and chairs, beautifully upholstered.

Everything in place.

As he headed to the stairs, Douglas could hear the housekeeper rattling around in the kitchen towards the back of the property.

On the middle floor were three expansive rooms and a bathroom. One room was a study. One wall had a fixed book cupboard with glass frontage, containing what looked like a collection of rare old books. In front of the bay windows stood a massive oak desk. The computer had been taken away by the police. Douglas checked the drawers. A few notepads and a leather document wallet that held a few bank cards, a driving licence, and a passport remained.

Items of interest, no doubt.

Douglas took the wallet and headed to the door. He scanned the book cabinet. As he passed, a bookmark from one of them caught his eye. He opened the glass door and pulled out the book that had a cloth cover. The old English typeface was barely readable. He opened the book at the page and realised it was a photograph. As the book fully opened, something else fell to the floor—another picture.

He picked them up to look closer. One had a group of five men, dressed in khaki military uniforms, holding rifles, posing next to a dead lion. Douglas couldn't help but tut his tongue. He instantly recognised Eric Lynch. One of the other men was familiar too.

Was that Joel Hopkins?

He was sure it was. He scanned the other faces but couldn't place any of the others.

He switched to the other photograph—three men posing with a dead elephant on some sun-drenched African plain.

A different hunting trip at another time, judging by the clothing. Eric looked different, unshaven. And next to him, Joel Hopkins. Douglas was sure it was him now. The shot was clearer. Then, he recognised another one of the men: Amaete Gonji.

"Hazelle! I found something!"

Chapter 18

The photographs and wallet Douglas had discovered, along with an open map of South England, were spread out on the table in the dining room. Hazelle's laptop stood open alongside.

The map had red pen marks of the murder locations. The golf course near Weybridge, Banstead Wood, and the building site in Ealing.

Hazelle studied the photos. "So clearly more than just working for the same company, this puts two of our murder victims together—where do you think this was taken?"

"Well, it looks like somewhere in Africa to me. That's one big continent though," Douglas replied.

"Fits in with those symbols the killer has been leaving, and at least gives us some starting point."

"Yes, we need to chase the semiotic expert."

Douglas flipped through Eric's British passport and went straight to the stamp pages.

"New York, Colombia, Chicago—Mauritius, Bangkok. Very nice. He got around—and Nairobi."

"More likely to be safari hunting there?"

"Yes, indeed," Douglas said, slowly. "I'll make some calls, see if I can get the flight manifests."

"What about asking Konrad? He might be able to—"

"It's okay. I'll speak to him," he said tactfully. "What would be good is seeing the police records of any other interviews with known friends and relatives of the victims."

"Yes, I'll see if I can get them," she said.

"Great. We need to start digging into the victims' backgrounds more—also any records of locals and neighbours' interviews. Someone must have seen something. And the semiotic update, if possible?"

While Hazelle picked up her mobile phone, Douglas took his and walked through the house to the front door before pulling up an old colleague's number.

After a few rings, a voice answered. "Alan Kettering speaking."

"Alan, it's Douglas Brown."

"Doug? Well, well. What's happening with you? How's retirement?"

"It's postponed at the moment, but it was going fine. Listen, can you do something for me?"

"Oh, that old chestnut? And I thought you just wanted to hear my silky voice."

***

Nearly an hour later, back inside Eric Lynch's house, the housekeeper brought in a silver tray with coffee and two cups.

"Very much appreciated, thank you," Doug said, with a broad smile. "We'll be out of your hair soon."

"That's no problem. Call if you need anything more," she said, before disappearing. Douglas glanced out of the room. Hazelle was wandering up and down the hallway, continually speaking into her phone, getting nowhere by the sound of it.

Douglas took out his notepad and stared at his wild scribbles. His old friend, Kettering, was one of his closest colleagues back in his Met days. Going through his contact seemed like a faster route to getting the manifests.

And those manifests had eventually come up with gold.

Joel Hopkins, Amarete Gonji, and Eric Lynch had all travelled to Nairobi Jomo Kenyatta before changing to Mombasa around the same dates in March, around seven months before.

So they went hunting, some old boys network, killing animals; the bastards. Did Konrad know this? Douglas poured himself a black coffee and sipped. He momentarily wondered if there was any brandy in the drinks cabinet to spice it up. A 'wobbly coffee' as the Navy boys called it.

The victims all knew each other; that was the key; they all went off on some hunting trip together. So, what was that telling him?

He picked up his mobile and called Konrad.

"I'm onto something I think. Just giving you an update."

"Oh, the ID of the killer?"

"Not quite. There's evidence that Hopkins, Gonji, and your brother went on a hunting trip in Africa. Do you know much about that?"

"No, not really. I mean, my brother went hunting all over the place."

"Right, well it seems worthwhile investigating further," Douglas reasoned.

"I disagree. That murderer is here in the UK. In and around London probably. You need to focus everything here, Douglas."

"But surely if there's some relevance to all the victims—"

"There's no relevance to the fact they went on holiday. What else have you got?"

Douglas gritted his teeth, his irritation rising.

"We're chasing a few other routine items but—"

"Keep in touch, Doug. Anything that comes up call me but focus on catching the killer here, in England." Konrad hung up.

Doug tossed his phone on the table and swore under his breath.

What just happened? There was a subtle change in Konrad's voice as soon as Africa was mentioned, and then there was his dismissive attitude. What was he hiding?

From the hallway, Hazelle's footsteps grew louder, and she entered the room, looking equally frustrated as he was.

"Nothing more from any other friends of the victims. They claim not to know anything. The SIO never got anywhere with that, and there's no update," she said, referring to the Senior Investigating Officer.

"Right," Douglas replied, distracted.

"The semiotics expert is Sarah Whitehead. She's at lunch. I can give you her number to call back?" Hazelle looked at Douglas, concerned. "Are you okay?"

"Hmm, oh, fine." Douglas considered telling Hazelle the conversation he just had but decided against it.

"There's another thing. I need to go home for a day or so. A personal matter," she added.

"No, that's fine. Coffee there, have some." He gestured at the pot.

"Thanks. Don't mind if I do."

Doug stood up.

"Listen, Hazelle. I'm going to have another search around before we leave."

"Need a hand?"

"No. You finish your coffee. Gather everything up to leave, if you could?"

Douglas headed upstairs to the top floor that Hazelle had searched. He needed to satisfy himself that every nook had been checked. He walked into the master bedroom and stood for a moment, looking around. It had been left immaculately tidy. One wall had an extensive inbuilt wardrobe, and two identical bedside cabinets flanked the double bed. On the wall opposite, a line of what looked like original framed paintings.

He headed for the wardrobe and opened up the first set of doors. There was a line of around ten tailored suits and expensive-looking shirts. Douglas started checking the pockets of each one. He closed the doors and moved to the next set of doors. This time, a more varied row of tweeds; what looked like hunting suits and game hunting jackets. He found nothing in those either then spotted a travel bag tucked away deep at the back of the wardrobe.

He pulled it out. Inside, were what looked like the remnants of some recent trip: several pairs of knee-length shorts, a couple of combat trousers, underwear packed in a washbag. In one of the outside pockets, he saw a business card that had wedged itself deep and managed to fish it out between his thumb and forefinger.

It was black both sides and had 'Amina Café' in an elaborate typeface with a coffee cup logo, followed by: 'Jasiirada Chula, Banjuno Islands, Somalia'.

He stared at it, his mind racing.

The flight manifest that led to Mombasa. This must have been their destination; he was sure of it. His thoughts returned to Konrad, shutting him down on pursuing that Africa lead.

Something clicked, deep down, and he had the strongest feeling he was on the right track now.

Douglas slipped the card into his wallet and finished his search. He had made a decision.

Downstairs, Hazelle had packed up their belongings and was ready to go.

"Find anything?"

"No. Let's get going."

Chapter 19

The ferry was an oblong rusty block with square holes for windows. The crate looked like its best years were behind it, the patchwork of repairs showing how many times it had needed serious attention.

But it was floating, that was the main thing, Douglas thought wearily.

A few locals eyed him suspiciously, but he hadn't had any problems so far. He rubbed his weary eyes. Why the hell had he come here? As far as long shots go, this one was way out there. Louise, he just needed to keep reminding himself it was for Louise. Everything he was doing was for her, but that didn't make the call that he was taking a trip to Kenya any easier.

He had kept the details vague. No mention of the hellish ten or so hours drive North to the Somalian border, after two flights to get to Mombasa. Nor did he mention to Louise anything about boat trips to Somalia islands. It would just be too worrying for her.

It was worrying for him. Douglas repeatedly questioned whether he was doing the right thing coming here, but he couldn't shake the feeling that the answer was here.

He felt his age, past sixty. At least he hadn't had to drive on that relentless journey that never seemed to end. That particular privilege was saved for Rab, his hired guide who had gladly taken his dollars. Douglas had tried to get broken sleep in the back, but it was near impossible, the heat and bumpy roads keeping rest at bay. Rab had shouted for him to lie low several times when passing through certain towns not deemed safe.

The scrubland and beaches of Jasiirada Chula, the most significant of the Bajuni islands in terms of population, grew more prominent on the horizon, and their boat was soon manoeuvring towards a wooden dock. The other passengers were already positioning themselves at the exit, clutching large bags of belongings and food. By the time Douglas had stepped off onto the pier, the crowd had gobbled up any waiting taxis. Several men gestured and shouted at Douglas, waving for him to buy trinkets at their makeshift stall. He waved them off and kept walking past rows of shacks and half derelict buildings. A motorbike sped past, with more shouts from two young men riding on it. Douglas jumped back, startled, but then saw one of them waving as the bike bounced around the potholes.

After a few metres, the waft of cooking food teased Douglas as he walked through an alley of various stalls. A row of multi-coloured, three-storey buildings came into view, including his hotel. He hoped they had received his messages because there had been no response before he had left for the airport.

The building looked old and run down like most of the town, long neglected by the central government. Douglas hadn't read too much, but the civil war, followed by UN occupation until '95, had caused massive fracturing across the country. This hotel looked like someone had built it expecting the tourist industry to start booming here, and then when the political unrest in Somalia got worse, their dreams fell apart like the government.

Douglas stepped inside the hotel, standing under the ceiling fan for a few moments, that slight breeze felt like a cold beer in the park. That thought reminded him to get one.

"Yes, sir? You are Mr. Brown?"

That was almost music to his ears.

The proprietor seemed friendly enough, perched behind a counter. Behind him, pigeon-hole shelves housed keys that dangled lifelessly.

"I am indeed."

The man grinned and pushed over a dusty register book.

"Good, good. I am Mali. Sign you in, and I show you room."

"Not busy at the moment?" Douglas asked, looking down at the sparse register. He turned the page back and scanned the previous bookings. The names looked like they were all Somalian or at least African.

"No. Very quiet. Not many visitors here at all. The war—" he stopped as if no other explanation was needed.

After checking in, Mali took Douglas's suitcase directly to Room 1, opposite the hotel reception desk.

"Will I be able to get food and something to drink?" Douglas asked, hopefully.

"Of course. We have small restaurant." Mali gestured towards the back of the building. "We will take good care of you, Mr. Brown."

"I hope so," Douglas replied quietly.

"I'm afraid there's no alcohol due to Somalia being a Muslim country."

"Ah, right. Yes, of course," Doug replied, disappointed.

He went inside his room, thanked Mali and shut the door and looked around. He was relieved to see a bed with a mosquito net. His years in Hong Kong had made him loathe the little bastards.

A sink with a dripping tap.

Not so good.

Although it was a far cry from the Marriot he was using back in England, it felt like a luxurious island in a sea of turbulence after his arduous journey. He fell back on the bed and closed his eyes.

Chapter 20

Douglas woke up with a lurch and groaned out loud. After a few moments of groggy confusion, he remembered where he was. He sat up from the same position he had fallen asleep in and looked down at the same shirt and slacks he had travelled in. After a shower and a change into a fresh short sleeve shirt and three-quarter length shorts, Douglas stepped out of his room into an empty reception area.

With fresh eyes, he was able to take in his surroundings in a clearer light.

He walked through the back of the building, past various doors until he arrived in a games room with a well-worn pool table. He heard voices through an open doorway. He stepped through onto a veranda that looked out across nothing but scrubland and a few concrete blockhouses.

"Mr. Brown!" His hotel concierge was brimming with morning enthusiasm and clearly happy to see Douglas recovered.

"We waited to cook, but you were asleep, Mr. Brown."

He gestured at a young woman who wore a pinny around an Arsenal football shirt, who Douglas assumed was the cook.

"Yes, sorry I was knackered—er very tired. Hungry now, though, starving."

"Good—good. Please, sit down."

Doug did so.

"So we have sabaayad, muqmad iyo ukun. This is flatbread with eggs

and beef or sweet potato and feta frittata. Then there is malawah, a
Somali sweet bread. Anjero, which is sourdough pancakes; cambabuur,
this is crepes with saffron, cumin and garlic."

Douglas felt overwhelmed with choice.

"Hmm, it all sounds great. The flatbread thing sounds great, please
and one to take away. Is that okay?"

"Yes."

"Thanks and lots of coffee, please."

The woman nodded and left.

"So, how's life here? Quiet?"

"Yes, very much last few months. Bajuni people only want freedom
from Somalian government and own land. Many times, they come and
take. Many of our people lost." Mani's face fell into an expression of
anger, just for a moment, then sadness.

Douglas nodded slowly. "Must have been some tough times."

"Yes, yes."

The woman came with coffee.

"Thank you, just what the doc ordered."

Douglas asked about the island, Mani's story, then broached his true
intentions.

"Have you seen this man at all?" Douglas pulled out a photo of Eric
Lynch and placed it on the table.

Mani picked the photo up and scowled at it. "Possibly, all you white
men look very similar," he said with a chuckle.

Douglas took out a photo of Joel. "What about him?"

Mani picked it up. "I— I don't know, sorry, my friend."

The third photo Douglas passed across the table was a photo of Gonji.

"Ah. Now, this man I remember," he said, picking up the photo. "He
was good fun, liked to dance."

"Do you know what they were doing here? Were they hunting?"

Mani's expression changed from cheerful to surprised.

"No, no. I'm sorry. I don't know." He stood up suddenly, avoiding eye contact.

"I will check your breakfast, sir," he added before leaving,

Douglas looked up at him, surprised, and offered a weak smile.

"Thank you."

Odd. Douglas hadn't expected that reaction.

After breakfast, Douglas left the hotel with a backpack, water bottle, the extra flatbread he'd ordered and went to get more supplies from a store down the street. He filled up with dried fruit and nuts, bananas, apples, fritters, and two large bottles of water. He asked the woman in the store if she had seen any of the men in his photos. She looked at each one and shook her head politely.

"Do you know where I can go hunting, near here?" he asked.

She frowned at him, the smile dropping from her face.

"Near here, Jasiirad Qarsoon is the only place." She spat on the ground as she said the name.

"Is there a problem at the island?" he asked her directly.

"It is cursed. Do not go there."

"Why?"

"Cursed," she repeated.

"I need to go. Is there no one?"

The woman thought for a moment. "Maybe fisherman. But maybe not."

Douglas headed off to the small harbour where he had come in the day before. The term 'harbour' was a bit of a stretch. It consisted of just a wooden jetty, a handful of boats and a few small buildings around it. Further along, there was a stretch of beautiful beach, and there were more fishing boats pulled up onto the pristine white sand. One of the fishermen sorting out his nets called over. Douglas walked up.

"Your boat for hire? Rent?"

The thin, older man nodded. "Yes, yes. Where you go? Ten dollars or a thousand shillings for one day."

Douglas took out his money.

"Take me to Jasiirad Qarsoon."

The fisherman looked concerned. "No. I cannot."

Douglas groaned out loud with frustration. "God's sake. No one wants to go there?"

"Can I hire your boat? Buy it even?"

"My livelihood."

"Of course—let me pay you well. I want to go for a few hours—but a day would be best. I'll give you fifty US dollars. That's a good and fair price, wouldn't you say? I will bring it back to you." Douglas took the banknotes out and held them in his hand.

The man looked hesitant; his eyes darting to the cash in Douglas's hand. Finally, he nodded, taking the money and stuffing it into his pocket.

Twenty minutes later, Douglas was gunning out to sea, the hull of the small boat bouncing on the waves. He navigated his hired motorboat diagonal to the rising tides so as not to get caught or capsize.

He was glad to be on track, and it felt now that he was finally closing in on the truth behind the gruesome murders.

Chapter 21

Douglas cut the engine and drifted as close as he could to the beach before climbing over into the shallow water. He pulled the boat onto the sand and took out his backpack with a satisfied sigh. It felt good to be outside, breathing in the fresh sea air after being stuck on planes, buses and cars for most of his journey.

The island certainly had a feeling of desolation. The scrubland was hedged by a twisted, dark tree line that led inland, interspersed with overgrown grass and shrubs. Douglas walked alongside it for a few metres, looking through the trees until he came to some natural trail and turned into it, pushing past some of the low hanging branches.

After five minutes of walking, through the cluster of plants and small trees in front of him, he could see a glimpse of blackened buildings.

He began to quicken his pace, pushing past a bush until he came out in a clearing where a cluster of small buildings lay in charred ruins.

His stomach churned with disappointment at the sight.

What information was he going to get from this place now?

Douglas circled the perimeter of the small village taking photographs. In the centre was what looked to have been the main lodge, now a blackened husk, along with seven small chalets. None of the buildings had escaped what must have been a raging fire.

Had the smoke been seen by passing boats or the main island?

Douglas tried to guess how long ago the fire might have happened.

Months, for sure. A year?

He gingerly stepped around the chalets on the blackened ground and peered inside one of them. The charred bones of the wood rafters had caved in and lay in broken chunks on a mound of debris. There were remnants of mattress springs and a skeleton of a wardrobe.

He took a few photographs, then moved along to the next chalet. Each was the same story. All burned out completely. Nothing left to give him an idea of what went on here.

He headed to the main building. There were concrete steps up to a long veranda that was covered in chunks of blackwood and debris. Douglas stepped through it slowly and went inside. The roof had caved in, and everything had burned into a pile of ash. In the centre, a stone chimney stood alone, like a crumbling black monolith reaching for the roofless sky.

After an hour, Douglas had found nothing more. He sat away from the ruins and ate some food under the shade of a tree.

What did this tell him? He had come here hoping for answers, some clue as to what might be behind the murders and had found nothing.

He continued walking inland, mopping his brow in the intense heat. He checked his watch. He should get back. Douglas turned to return and caught sight of a fence just beyond a clump of trees. He walked closer and beat back some of the overgrowth that had taken over to get a better look. He saw the fence was well built and around five metres high. It ran as far as the eye could see, disappearing down the brow of a hill, then reappearing in the distance.

If Douglas didn't know better, he would have thought he was in some enclosed camp. He glugged down some water and set off back to the boat.

Chapter 22

Axmed Hamza stared out across the skyline of London, a myriad of lights shining out in the dark on the monolithic buildings that dominated the view. The winding Thames river was shimmering in the moonlight like a glass snake through the dark urban undergrowth.

As much as he hated being in this country, forced here to seek vengeance, Hamza had to admit the view was to die for. He focused on the adjacent glass-fronted building while the wind buffeted against his face. The crystal blue square of the swimming pool on the penthouse roof was covered by a structural glass roof that curved over it like a protective pearl shell. Just outside, a terrace with a bar now closed up and several bamboo tables and chairs.

He stepped forward and stood upon the ledge of the 300-metre high building, glancing down at the steady stream of traffic below. Then, with a sharp intake of breath, he spread his arms and jumped, pushing himself well clear of the building.

The winged suit he was wearing cut through the rushing wind, bringing Hamza closer to the target building. As he glided in fast to the terrace, he pulled his cord. The chute opened, slowing his descent, but he could not avoid the table and chairs. He gritted his teeth as his feet slammed into the chairs, knocking them over.

He pulled at the small chute, getting it down and under control. Once he had his weight on top of it and the wind was no longer trying to tear it free, he froze, listening for any sound from inside the building.

All he could hear were wind gusts and the sound of the city far below. There should be no one in the penthouse suite; as with all his victims, he had done his research, watched and followed Lustig for days to find the best place to get to him.

Getting past the security of the building next to his and getting to the roof had proven invaluable. The height difference was just enough for the base jump to be possible, and then it was just a case of keeping a close eye on the weather reports for a favourable day when Lustig was out.

He walked over to the sheltered part of the terraced garden, parachute in his arms and laid it out flat, sorting the lines and fabric before repacking into his bag.

He found a suitable place to conceal it, just behind the closed bar and then went back, putting the table and chairs back in place. He checked the time. His victim would be home soon. Now they seemed to know that he was coming for them; things were getting slightly more problematic. He liked the challenge, though; easy prey was not satisfying.

Finding the right place to ambush Lustig had been a challenge. The businessman had hired a couple of hard men in suits who Hamza was sure he could have taken out without problems, but he liked to think of himself as a fine blade, only cutting out the rot.

Lustig seemed to feel safe once he was in his penthouse apartment. His fortress.

The security guards would come, escort him upstairs and then wait for him outside. The security system on the apartment was advanced, too much to overcome. Still, it only covered the main access points and interior rooms.

Sitting quietly, crouched in a dark area of the terrace, Hamza knew all he had to do now was wait. Wait until his victim came home and switched it all off.

Hamza closed his eyes and chanted quietly, remembering those for whom he sought revenge. A light spittle of rain began to fall, like a fine mist, and the killer shivered as he thought of his homeland.

Then a change of light across the terrace floor snapped him back to the present.

Lustig was home.

Having watched him for a few weeks now, Hamza knew the routine was always the same. The businessman came back from work, had dinner, watched the TV, or worked on his computer, then headed to bed between 11:30 pm and midnight.

On Tuesdays and Thursdays, he would swim. On Fridays, he would stay out late or not come back at all. Today was a Tuesday.

The killer walked up to the bi-folding doors to the terrace. He took out his tools and expertly picked the lock, sliding open the doors silently. He could already hear the splashing as his victim unwound in the pool. Hamza padded silently up to the doorway that led to the pool and stood there, watching him swim, enjoying the calm moments before the inevitable terror.

He turned and padded through the open plan kitchen and looked into a side room. It was a pool room, in the centre a large table and bar in the corner. He walked up to the rack containing the pool cues and picked one up, weighing it in his hands. Then Hamza pulled out a large hunting knife and began methodically sharpening the tip into a sharp point.

When he was satisfied with the point, Hamza headed back to the pool area. Again he stood in the doorway watching for a while before opening a pouch on his trousers and gradually pulling out a large net.

He waited for his victim to reach the closest side of the pool and then when he switched his body for the return length, Hamza quickly strolled out into the pool area. He walked alongside Lustig who was swimming a few feet from the edge, watching him as he smacked the water with his arms doing a front crawl.

As Lustig was halfway through his length, Hamza leaned the makeshift spear on the wall and held the net wide with both hands. He threw it just ahead of Lustig's trajectory.

The net splayed open, then fell onto the swimmer, sinking over the water and his body.

Lustig was soon fully entangled, making it worse as he continued to power through the pool without realising what was happening, wrapping the net around himself. He grunted out loud, stopped swimming and then began to struggle, splashing around as he tried to free himself.

"Was zur Hölle?"

Hamza picked up the cue and with one practised swoop raised it high above his head and stabbed it with full force at Lustig.

A gargled cry echoed off the glass roof.

Dark blood gushed from the wound, polluting the pool in deep red clouds. Lustig flailed around in the water, and just for a moment, Hamza spotted, with satisfaction, a deep gouge in Lustig's shoulder.

He raised the cue again and jabbed the point straight into Lustig's neck. Another cry of pain.

As he pulled it back out, a jet of blood sprayed across the surface of the clear blue water. Lustig's animalistic wails shrieked to an unbearable pitch.

Hamza hit the cue over his victim's head again and again until the cries faded and the only sound was the wet slapping sound of the repeated blows.

Then he stopped, breathless, watching the lifeless body drift, face down. The clear blue water was deep red around the body, a pinkish gradient slowly spreading.

Hamza tossed the cue into the pool with a splash and headed back to the terrace. He picked up his chute, taking his time strapping it on. Then he walked to the edge, facing away from the prevailing wind and jumped into the darkness.

Chapter 23

"Douglas? What the hell is happening? You should have returned my calls. There's been another homicide. Michael Lustig, tossed up like a kipper by his penthouse pool. I suggest you get the fuck down there."

Douglas had deliberately called his home landline to hide where he was and sighed at Konrad's tone. His dislike for his old colleague was expanding like a balloon every time they spoke. "Slow down. Where's this murder?"

"Central London. Your investigation work has been piss poor. I've still got no idea on where or who this fucking psycho is—and another thing, you're supposed to be working with Hazelle and she's not heard a peep from you all fucking week—"

"Believe it or not I'm working on it Konrad! Now, if you'll—"

"I don't believe it. I'm withholding any further payments to you until there's a breakthrough! You can get off your arse, call Hazelle and get down to London."

"You can't—"

The line went dead.

Douglas was about to ring back but decided not to. Instead he dialled home.

"Hi love, it's me."

"Doug. Lovely to hear you. When are you coming home?"

"Soon, I promise." He felt his heart sink. He was nowhere near solving this it seemed and now the cash was frozen. He was failing her badly.

"How are you doing, hon?"

"Ah, well I'm okay but the pain is much worse some mornings. It's getting bad—"

He held his eyes closed as she spoke.

"Oh god," Douglas whispered under his breath. "I'm doing everything I can—the treatment?"

"It's almost finished. Will they be sending another prescription?"

"I'll—I'll get onto them."

"Are you alright?" she asked. It was typical of her to always be thinking of others. Totally unselfish.

"Yes, we'll get through this together. I'm up against a wall with the job at the moment, but I promise we'll get through this."

"Okay." She sounded so trusting it made Douglas feel sick. He would deal with this by any means.

After the call, Douglas sat down at the edge of his bed and held his head in his hands.

Get a grip, Doug.

He took out his wallet and checked his currency notes and pulled out the business card he had found in Eric's house for the Amina Café.

It was somewhere to check out at least. He left the hotel and wandered around the streets until he found the café bar, which was essentially a concrete block but the owner had managed to create a saloon-style atmosphere with sofas and low chairs set around coffee tables. He ordered a tea, sat down and looked around. Behind the makeshift counter on the wall was what seemed to be a collage of photographs.

The proprietor came over with a pot and asked him where he was from.

"Just visiting."

A local man, probably the same age, nodded and smiled then sat down nearby.

"You go to island?" He gestured in the general direction of the sea.

"You know something about that?" Douglas asked, looking across to the doorway as a young couple entered the bar. The light outside was fading fast and hanging Christmas lights that were strung around the walls flickered to life.

"My brother—he the fisherman you hired the boat from."

He dragged his chair next to the man.

"You want a stronger drink?" he asked Douglas.

"I'd love a beer. Didn't think it was allowed?"

The man spoke to the bar owner and Douglas's tea was soon replaced by a bottle of beer.

"Yes, I took a look at that island. Everyone seems very scared of the place. I don't suppose you're gonna tell me anything about it? What that burned out lodge is all about?" Douglas asked, hopefully.

"Many locals go missing over the years. During the war we had refugees go to the Somalian mainland, but this was different. They just disappear." He waved his hand like a magician conjuring a spell.

"Who disappeared?"

"Mostly men but sometimes woman too—"

"So, they went missing and you have an idea of what happened to them?"

He shook his head. "Only that rich men go to island—they hire bad Somalians. We close our eyes to it. I'm ashamed to say. Nothing we can do or we endanger our lives."

Douglas nodded. "I understand, right. And the burned out lodge?"

"I don't know. Someone set fire to it about six, seven months ago."

Douglas mulled that over for a few moments, then stood up.

"I need to go to the bathroom." Douglas followed the sign and stepped into a small grimy room with no roof. He took a leak then washed his hands and headed back to the café, dejected. He was losing the case and was heading home with nothing.

The noise level seemed to increase as more customers came inside, talking and laughing. In response, the barman went to the back and disappeared around a stack of crates while Douglas's gaze fell on the photo collage behind the bar. There must have been hundreds of images, mainly Africans but also what must have been the rare visits from tourists. Naturally the few photos with Caucasian faces stood out, and as Douglas stared, he swore he could see some familiar features. Struggling to get a clear vision he stood up and moved around the wood plank bar.

"Bloody hell!" He couldn't believe his eyes.

A photograph of Konrad Lynch posing alongside Joel Hopkins, Eric Lynch, Will Leung, Amaete Gonji and two other men he didn't recognise. They were in a group, arms around each other, beaming at the camera.

So, Konrad knew the victims?

The barman came back carrying a crate of soda bottles.

"This photo—do you remember these men?" Douglas asked.

The barman put the crate down on the floor and came and looked.

"Yes, yes—was months ago—maybe a year? They came here only once. Had many drinks one evening like celebrating something. But I didn't talk to them.

"Thank you. Can I take this photograph? It's important for a police investigation."

The café owner hesitated, and Douglas pulled out his wallet and handed him a $10 bill. The café owner smiled, took down the photo and handed it to him.

"Come, have another drink my friend," the barman said, showing Douglas back to his seat.

Chapter 24

As he wheeled his suitcase out to a line of taxis outside Heathrow airport, his phone buzzed and vibrated with calls and messages. Douglas knew, without looking, that it would be Konrad, probably Hazelle as well.

He joined the taxi queue, ignoring the phone until he was in the back of a black cab.

Back to the shit pit and time to dance with the devil.

He had plenty of messages from Konrad, two from Louise and five from Hazelle. He called Louise first, told her he was back safe and promised to get up to Scotland as soon as he could. She was weak but stable.

"I'm going to sort this money out by the end of today. You won't have to worry about the treatment stopping anymore."

After the call, Douglas texted Konrad to say he would be at his house in an hour then gazed out of the window at the passing sprawl of London's suburbs, his mind clear of all thoughts.

***

The front door, black and polished, surrounded by ivy, swung open. Konrad stood, unshaven, features seemingly deeper set than when Douglas had last seen him. He donned an old fashioned cardigan that made him look like a '70s granddad.

"You've been abroad? You look tanned, and there's been no fucking sun here." He was gruff, morose, but surprisingly not angry considering the last few calls and texts.

"Care to explain this?"

Douglas had taken out the photo from the bar in Jasiirada Chula and held it up directly in front of Konrad's stony face. All the anger and fight in Konrad seemed to fade.

"You went to Somalia then? You'd better come in."

In the study, Konrad poured a large Bourbon and gestured to Douglas with the bottle. He declined, staring at Konrad with expressionless eyes.

Konrad took a gulp and sat down in an Edwardian style chair by the double windows. He gazed out into the garden as he spoke.

"We were all at Oxford, that's how we first met."

"Just to clarify who we are talking about," Douglas interjected.

"Yes, of course. The recent homicide victims you've been investigating. Eric Lynch, my brother. Joel Hopkins, Amaete Gonji, Will Leung, Michael Lustig. There's also Ralph Sanderson, who's still alive and has hired guards round the clock."

Douglas flipped through his notepad and scribbled down Sanderson's name. He didn't want to interrupt Konrad.

"But it was many years later at a reunion we began to network, form our own little chapter—"

"Like the Masons?"

Konrad snorted with derision. "Sure—well we did business deals, but mainly it was leisure activities together."

"Hunting on Safari?"

"Yes—at first. It was a regular thing for years. Some illegal ones too."

Douglas tutted.

Konrad turned to Douglas for the first time, holding back tears. Douglas wasn't expecting that.

"That's the least of it—" He drained his glass. "I can't remember who suggested it, but they had a contact who organised this kind of thing—they organised everything with the—prey. Pretty lawless over there, especially if there was good money on the table."

"So what were you hunting?" Douglas felt confused, frustrated.

Konrad stood up and went to the drinks cabinet and poured another.

"Humans, Douglas. We hunted people." He downed the golden liquid in one swoop.

Douglas stood stunned, unable to speak.

"There was incredible pressure to go along," Konrad added as if this made it slightly more acceptable.

"You hunted and killed people?" Douglas managed to spit out, still struggling to comprehend what he was hearing.

"I didn't personally kill anyone, Douglas. But I was involved, and now we're all paying the price."

Douglas held both his hands on the back of his head, staring at Konrad in disbelief.

Konrad put his glass down as if finally done with the booze.

"Tremendous pressure to be part of it. Everyone knew everyone's business, all the dirty little secrets. Why do you think the investigation into Oak Castle didn't go anywhere? There were countless other schemes planned, but the main point is everyone had dirt on everyone else."

"So you felt compelled to go? Hunting for humans?"

Konrad took a handkerchief and blew his nose. "I was on that island, stalking through the trees with my shotgun. There were"—Konrad began to weep—"women too."

"How many were there? Victims of your murderous friends I mean—"

"Six, it should have been seven but I, I couldn't—I had a clear shot, through the trees but I couldn't do it. I caught a glimpse as he jumped down behind some rocks."

"What happened to him?"

"When they saw me hesitate, the guide said not to worry. They would take care of it."

86

"And the other victims?"

"There were constant gunshots. When we reassembled at the lodge, everyone claimed they had trapped and killed their—prey."

"Why didn't you tell me this from the start, put me on the right trail?"

"I needed you to find the killer. Would his motives have made a difference? I mean even with this information are you any closer to knowing who he is or where he is?"

Douglas slumped down onto a chaise lounge positioned in the corner.

"I knew you were a bastard, but—this is incredible. You're a detective superintendent for fuck's sake!"

"You don't understand the power of these people. They're everywhere, and they can destroy your life with the wave of a hand. How was I supposed to say no?"

"Conspiracies now, Konrad? I would have thought you better than that."

Konrad shook his head as if tutting a child.

"Naive, Douglas, you don't know the half of it—"

Douglas stood up, the shock now giving way to rage.

"So I've been chasing my tail all this time?" Douglas shouted. "This information could have put me on the right path. My wife is fucking dying, Konrad."

Konrad looked away. "I'll fix that—the money—you need the treatment."

Douglas shook his head in disbelief.

"How will I take your money now? I need to inform your superiors."

"You need to save your wife, Douglas. If I get arrested now, that's all over. Just hear me out. He's correctly targeted everyone so far. He got Michael a few days ago, as you know; just me and Ralph Sanderson left now. Help me find him before he kills me, Douglas."

Douglas sniggered. "I should wish him good hunting. Leave him to it."

"Remember, the contract is to find the killer's identity. I'll go to my superiors with the details when you've done that. Then you can save your wife," he added, quietly.

"You're a real piece of shit." Douglas almost spat on the floor.

Chapter 25

The rain pelted the windscreen, making it difficult to get a clear view of the pillared house set behind a low wall. The exterior lights helped, as Sanderson had his house lit up like a Christmas tree.

Obviously, he was worried about security and fully aware that a killer was on the loose with Sanderson and Konrad in his sights. With no chance of going to the police, he must be petrified, Douglas thought.

He deserved it, of course.

Hazelle hadn't spoken much since he picked her up, then Doug told her about Konrad's confession. She had almost broken down into tears, then after composing herself, said, "You cut me out of the investigation."

"It was a lead, and Somalia is still a dangerous place. I didn't want to put you in any—"

"You needn't have worried about that. I can look after myself."

"I'm sure you can. Well, let's be extra careful tonight."

"He's coming out," Hazelle said.

Douglas saw Sanderson step out of the door and look around.

"Well spotted. That someone with him?"

A bigger man went out first and had a good look around, then nodded to Sanderson in the doorway.

"Yeah. His security?"

The two men went to the white Bentley Continental Coupe parked outside the garage. Sanderson threw a gym bag in the boot and then got in the driver's seat. The security guard got in the passenger's before the lights came on.

"Alright, we're in business."

Douglas followed at a distance, keeping well back. They would be looking for tails or anything suspicious.

"They'll see you," Hazelle said in a disapproving tone. Douglas slowed and let a car pull out in front of him and continued following at a distance.

After a ten-minute drive, Sanderson pulled into an exclusive looking leisure centre. Everyone had decided to come and work out judging by the packed car park.

"So he's checking in at the gym. Can't be that worried."

Douglas saw a space but was soon beaten by an old silver Mercedes.

"Shit!"

"There's one." Hazelle pointed to space in the next row.

"Thanks." Douglas pulled into it just in time to see Sanderson and the grunt disappear inside the front entrance.

"Guess they're workout buddies."

They waited an hour and twenty minutes before the men came out again and headed back to the same residence.

Douglas turned off his engine once they had pulled up down the street.

"I think that's it tonight. You should go home."

"Oh, not that again. I'm not going anywhere. Game of cards?"

"Suit yourself. Feel free to call me a grumpy old git, but I'm not playing cards."

"Git—"

***

The following day, Douglas and Hazelle had taken it in turns to watch; the house was quiet. Hazelle walked up the high street to get coffee and bagels.

There was no sign of Sanderson until the same time that evening. As Sanderson, along with his bodyguard, pulled out and headed up the road, a white van came to a stop a few metres ahead of Douglas's car.

"What have we here?" Douglas was about to pull out to follow Sanderson but hesitated.

"We're losing Sanderson."

The door opened, and a builder got out, looking at a piece of paper. He looked around, then headed up a pathway to a different house.

"No, don't think that is anyone to be concerned about."

Douglas had to lean heavy on the gas to catch up but soon saw the familiar tail lights indicate to turn into the leisure club. They parked and watched the two men go inside, as the night before.

"Are we wasting our time do you think?" Hazelle asked.

"It's the nature of our work—never really knowing if it's leading anywhere. You know that."

A Mercedes crawled around the corner and went past the rear of Douglas's vehicle. There was a flicker of recognition. He observed the car as it pulled into a spare space a few rows in front of them.

"That car—it was around yesterday."

"Are you sure? Could be a regular to the gym?"

They both looked at each other then back at the car to see who got out. They waited to see who the driver was, but after a few minutes, no one had got out.

"Who pulls into a car park and doesn't get out of their car?"

"Well, we didn't."

"Hmmm, exactly," Douglas replied.

"Take a note of his reg number and wait here."

"Where are you—"

Douglas was already out of the car, walking along the row of vehicles. Then he changed direction and headed parallel to the Mercedes before heading towards the passenger door.

He opened the passenger door quickly and leaned in to see a young Afro-Caribbean man with sharp cheekbones that made him look more Arabic than black.

Somalian?

He looked at Douglas, startled just for a moment then seemed to be assessing him. Douglas scanned inside the vehicle.

"Please don't be alarmed, sir. I'm security," Douglas said, in his most commanding voice.

On the passenger seat, right in front of him was a small shoulder bag with scattered notepad paper underneath along with a photo of what could have been Sanderson but was too obscured to be sure. There was a sleeping bag and scattered clothes on the back seats.

"Are you?" the man replied, quickly finding his composure.

"Can I ask what you're doing here?" Douglas continued, ignoring him.

"I waiting—for a friend." There was determination in his eyes.

"Really? Who's that?" Douglas pointed at the photo under the bag and went to grab it.

The man switched on the engine, still staring hard at Douglas, his hand reaching for the handbrake.

"Wait!" Douglas instinctively grabbed the bag and jumped back as the Merc reversed fast, almost hitting a parked vehicle directly behind. He sped off, screeching around the car park before the engine faded as it raced up the road.

Douglas walked back to the car and slipped into the passenger seat.

"I'm pretty sure that was him. You get the reg?"

"'Course. Already checking it out."

He opened the bag. A torch, wire cutters, screwdriver. A zip-up pouch.

Douglas felt his heart beating hard and realised he was excited. Was this the moment he could put this all to bed? Had he found his man?

"Do you have some gloves in there?" Douglas asked, nodding to the storage compartment.

"Funnily enough—" Hazelle pulled out a pack containing latex ones used to handle items at a crime scene and handed them to Douglas. After he slipped them on, he slowly unzipped the pouch.

He paused then inhaled and said, under his breath, "Bingo."

Chapter 26

"It's done as far as I'm bloody concerned," Douglas said with finality. "We have his car registration, a description—I'm ninety-nine per cent certain he had info on Sanderson on his car seat, and here..." Douglas threw the passport down on the table.

Douglas stared at Konrad defiantly.

"I have finally fulfilled my contract to find him."

Douglas gestured at the array of items on the table in front of them.

Konrad was sitting, cross-legged in his armchair. It was just him and Douglas, as Hazelle had gone to the hotel for a much-needed sleep.

"Yes, it looks like you have. I'll arrange your payment."

"Thank you. Surely this is all a police matter now, huh?" Douglas reasoned.

"I'll take care of that," he replied.

Douglas eyed him suspiciously. "You'll be telling them everything? Including your part in this squalid affair?"

"I will—I just want the killer taken care of before getting into all that mess."

"In what way?"

Konrad looked up at his old colleague with an offended frown. "What do you mean?"

"You intend to have him arrested by the police, don't you?"

Would Konrad have someone like that killed? It would tie up a huge problem for him, no doubt. Bury that story for good.

Konrad laughed. "I'm a Detective Super for Christ's sake. I wouldn't have someone killed."

Douglas wasn't sure he believed him.

"It wouldn't be the first time there was total corruption in the Met."

Konrad shook his head dismissively.

"Douglas, Douglas. Help me catch the bastard. Please—it's just me and Sanderson left on his fucking list." Konrad began to look desperate again.

"It's your mess. Why should I continue to risk my arse if you're not even going to bring in the Met to help you?"

"How long do we go back, Douglas? The seventies, the eighties?"

"What? Oh, in the Met—yeah—"

"It was rough, but we would never have believed how bad things would get, huh? The ever-increasing crime rate continued government cuts. It's no wonder we're in the shit as a country—a shadow of its former self."

Douglas sighed. He could tell where this was going, and he wasn't in the mood. He began buttoning up his coat.

"I'm leaving, Konrad. Please make that payment—my wife's life depends on it."

"What are you going to do? Louise, will she—?"

"I don't know. I'll do everything to make her life as comfortable as possible for as long as I can."

Konrad leaned back in his chair, his hands clasped together, his expression pensive. "Right now, she's getting the best treatment in the UK, but what if she was getting the best in the world?"

Chapter 27

In his car, Axmed Hamza rechecked his small backpack one more time. Pry bar, flashlight, binoculars, cable ties, night vision goggles, the box containing a vial of concentrated acid. Then there were two of his homemade circular explosive devices.

He checked his watch. Not long now.

Hamza thought back to how he had come to be in this cursed country. His parents and siblings, along with an estimated 200,000 other civilians, were wiped out by the government forces of Mohamed Siaad Barre's Somali National Army in the late 1980s.

Barre's campaign to destroy the opposition to his government was unrestrained. His bombers wiped out the city of Hargeisa, killing 40,000. His army rounded up farmers and families in the outlying villages and towns and murdered them, the flat red riverbeds of Malko-Durduro outside the city became their mass graves.

The 'Isaaq Genocide' or 'Hargeisa Holocaust' had become known as the forgotten genocide. A genocide that so far had attracted no international condemnation or even any criminal punishment.

Aged just ten, Hamza found himself part of a massive exodus to Ethiopia, where he was eventually recruited into the Somali Salvation Democratic Front, one of the many guerrilla movements opposing Barre and his dictatorship. Hamza's teen years became a blur of military training and the ways of death and revenge in which he excelled.

For five years he lived, breathed and trained with the guerrillas and was part of an offensive to take control of western districts. Eventually, the Barre Government was overthrown in 1991.

Although it was a challenging and sometimes brutal time for Hamza, having to deal with a life without comfort, he did meet Fawzia. She made all the pain and suffering a dimmed memory, and together they made plans for the future.

As the power vacuum created more fighting and turned Somalia into a 'failed state', the UN Peacekeeping forces moved in. Hamza and his new wife escaped the chaos on a boat to the Bajuni Islands where Fawzia had relatives, and for a few years, they were happy.

Happiness that would soon turn to horror.

Hamza was brought back to the present with a beep from his watch.

He left the car with his backpack, jumped over the low wall and headed into the darkness of the park. On the far side, a line of trees and bushes flanked Sanderson's residence. Hamza crouched in a hideaway and put down his bag. He took out the flashlight and cable ties and put them in his jacket pocket. Then he strapped the NVGs around his neck before carefully taking the vial of clear liquid and placing it in his breast pocket.

He checked the road, then his watch again and grabbed the pry bar and jumped over the wall onto the empty street and crossed over.

At a pavement cover, he leaned down and levered the pry bar into the slot and wrenched it open, revealing the electrical cables beneath. With gloved hands, he reached into his breast pocket and carefully took out the small bottle of clear liquid. Slowly, he unscrewed the lid, focusing all his concentration on it before pouring the vicious liquid over the cables. The smouldering began instantly as the acid ate away at the wires, dissolving them into charred husks. He looked up at Sanderson's house and watched with satisfaction as the lights inside quickly died. An alarm soon kicked into life, piercing the night air.

He replaced the cover and quickly retreated to his nearby hiding place, taking out his binoculars before shouldering his backpack.

Like a wasp nest poked into life, the house and front lawn outside was soon a hive of activity as two guards came outside with torches, one checking the electrical box while the other man scanned the gardens.

From his surveillance, Hamza knew there were at least two guards. One always stuck close to Sanderson. He had spotted another when he had moved one of the cars into the garage.

Now, through his binoculars, he spotted a third guard giving orders from the doorway.

They all knew he was coming, no doubt.

It was essential to focus and see this through now. That detective who approached him in the gym car park had taken him by surprise and taken his bag. They knew his identity now.

They would be finally closing in and he had to exact his revenge and quickly.

The alarm stopped, then the guards slowly retreated into the house. Hamza waited a few minutes, then headed across the quiet road to the low garden wall of Sanderson's house and into his grounds. He stealthily approached the house, taking care to remain hidden as much as he could but with the power out any CCTV would be down.

He crouched under a ground floor window, listened carefully, then took out a small circular explosive device from his bag and clamped it onto the glass.

He continued along the house wall and planted two more devices on the kitchen and dining room windows.

Still leaning against the wall, he checked his watch.

They should be here by now. This would screw it all up.

It was the pizza delivery judging by the sound of the approaching scooter. The high-pitched engine whined like a mosquito, then it lowered to a rumble and finally cut out.

Hamza counted the seconds, then heard the distant buzz of the doorbell. He rechecked his watch.

Come on!

There was a low murmur of talking at the door.

It needed to happen now.

And then the sound Hamza was waiting for as his homemade device timers finally ran out. A series of small explosions and shattered glass pierced the air.

He pulled out a pair of night-vision goggles and put them on, moving quickly to the nearest window where the shattered glass had blown inside. Smoke blew in cloud-like waves into the air. He elbowed a few intact shards and climbed inside the dark room. On the floor above, he could hear quick footsteps.

At least one of the guards would be left dealing with a very confused delivery driver. The others would be securing their boss in one of the upper rooms from what he could hear.

Slowly he crept along the corridor. The house had fallen silent again apart from the calm voice of the security guard at the front door, using his radio to call his colleagues. As he headed down the corridor to the front of the house, he could see the front door was still ajar, the heel of one foot keeping it open.

Silently, he approached. Through the crack, he could see the delivery driver lying face down, his hands behind his head.

The security guard, a barrel-chested man, stood over him with a pistol pointed at the terrified delivery driver.

Hamza shoulder barged open the door, grabbed the security guard by both shoulders and drove his knee hard up into his coccyx.

He cried out in pain, his pistol hitting the ground.

Keeping his hands firmly on his shoulders, Hamza pulled him backwards through the front doorway. His weight and the momentum threw him onto the tiled floor. There was a dull crack, and the guard groaned.

Hamza dropped one knee onto the guard's chest and rained several solid blows to his head, to make sure there was no getting back up in a hurry. He then rolled him onto his front, taking out two cable ties from his pocket and securing his hands behind his back. He then dragged the limp body back, so his feet were inside.

The delivery driver stayed in position, his hands still on his head.

"I know where you work; call the police, and I'll kill you," he whispered, then closed the door, not waiting for a response. Maybe it would work, perhaps not, but it should buy him some time.

He unclipped the radio and earpiece from the unconscious guard and then headed back into the dark house. He went past the main stairs into the kitchen, then took off his backpack and pulled out a long spring trap. He placed it down in line with the back door, careful to step on each side of the jagged drop jaws, and then slipped in the trigger pin.

Then he looked around and took a roll of kitchen towels off the food prep island and headed for the stairs.

Slowly he climbed, taking it step by step, looking up to the two floors above, unsure where Sanderson and his guards might be.

On the first floor, he padded from room to room in a clearing pattern and slowly realised they must be on the top floor above.

He started to unravel the kitchen roll, scrunching them up into balls before dropping them onto a pile on the carpet. Hamza produced a lighter from his combat trousers and set the small hill of paper towels on fire. He continued dropping more paper 'fuel' on the fire, and within seconds the corridor and stairwell began filling with smoke. The fire alarm quickly cut in, piercing the house with a high pitched beeping.

There was a crackle in his ear from the radio he had taken.

"Bravo Ten, you there? Is that a fire?!"

Hamza backed away from the fire into a side room as a glimpse of torchlight appeared on the steps, and watched as the first guard appeared, pistol drawn, followed by Sanderson and one behind him. They got to the landing, cautiously looking around, trying to see through the smoke with their torches.

Hamza looked around and unscrewed a bulb from a side lamp, then peeped out through the door to see them passing on the landing. As they descended the next flight of stairs, he crept to the landing banisters and dropped the bulb into the smokey darkness and quickly stepped back.

There was a 'tschhhh' sound from the bulb smashing on the ground floor below, and the men froze for a brief moment. Then the point man continued down the stairs. Hamza moved quickly across the landing, then descended behind the rear guard, who began to turn around.

Too late.

Hamza snaked an arm around his neck, gripped it hard and began dragging him back up the steps, his handgun clattering down the stairs. The guard desperately dug his fingers into Hamza's arm, vainly attempting to loosen the grip while his feet cart-wheeled, desperately trying to find balance.

Sanderson, realising what was happening, yelled in terror and fled downwards. At the bottom, the first guard quickly got in front of his boss, Sanderson, and pointed his flashlight with one hand while resting the other on top, aiming the handgun back up the stairs.

But the guard had no clear shot of Hamza, while he was shielded with his friend.

Hamza felt the guard's body go limp as he lost consciousness, the dead weight causing him to stumble and be exposed.

The loud crack of a gunshot rang out and a bullet whizzed past Hamza's shoulder. With gritted teeth, Hamza continued dragging the guard onto the landing and out of sight. He then rolled the unconscious guard over and secured his wrists with cable ties.

The guard shouted from the bottom of the stairs: "The police are on their way. You're trapped!" Through the smoke, his flashlight beam bounced around the hallway ceiling before switching off.

Hamza crouched in the darkness, wondering what to do. He was probably right, the police would be on route, and with one staircase he was effectively stuck.

He could not stop now. His revenge was so close to completion.

Quickly and silently, the killer moved into one of the bedrooms and closed the door behind him. Then he headed to the window, opened it wide and looked down at the ground, twenty feet away. He hauled himself onto the ledge and climbed out, hands grasping the drainage pipe. Keeping his body weight as close to it as possible, he slid down in stages, scraping his face against the pipe, then jumped the last ten feet and rolled on the lawn.

After a few deep breaths, he moved around the house and re-entered through the same window he had first come in. He crept up to the door and peeped out.

The guard intermediately turned on his flashlight to check the top landing, speaking into his radio, then he turned to his boss, Sanderson, who was out of sight.

"Stay where you are until the police get here, understand?"

"I wanna get out of here!" he replied with a hiss.

Hamza slowly pulled out a fixed blade knife from his sheath that was strapped around his calf and gripped it in his hand. He had so far tried to avoid unnecessary bloodshed, but this was war.

With a few swift strides, he was behind the guard in seconds.

He plunged the knife deep into the side of his neck, then pulled out the blade and stood back. As the guard screamed and gripped his palm over the spurting blood, Hamza turned to the terrified Sanderson and held a finger over his lips.

The guard sank to his knees, his cries turning to animalistic shrieks. The weapon and flashlight had now fallen onto the ground. Hamza kicked away the pistol, picked up the flashlight then wiped the blood from the knife on the guard's shoulder. He pointed the light at Sanderson's face as he stood in the kitchen doorway. Through the remains of the wispy smoke, Sanderson's illuminated face, set in a mask of abject horror, stared back at him.

"Please—" he whimpered, tears streaming down his face.

Then he cowed as Hamza made a sudden movement towards him as if shooing a cat.

Sanderson stared at him, puzzled, stepping back into the kitchen.

"Run! If you want to live," Hamza hissed. He held up his knife with a threatening glint. Behind him, the guard was whimpering for help.

Sanderson turned and bolted into the dark kitchen, towards the back door. As he reached it, there was a loud snap of metal.

"Aaarghhhhhhhhh!" His yell punctured through the house.

Hamza slowly walked into the kitchen and aimed the torch, revealing his victim bent over as he desperately attempted to wrench open the metal jaws that trapped his leg.

"What the fuck is this?" he screamed again. "Please—you fucking bastard—why? you fucking bast—"

Hamza sat down on a stool by the kitchen counter. In the distance, the whooping of sirens.

Sanderson's anger dissipated.

"Please—I didn't want to do it—it wasn't my idea—" His tone now pleading.

He continued trying to free himself, his efforts getting him nowhere as blood pooled on the kitchen floor from his wound.

"You still have to pay for your crimes, Mr. Sanderson. I wish I could stay longer."

He stood up and walked slowly towards his terrified victim, knife gripped in hand, ready to do his dark work.

Chapter 28

Douglas's mobile phone rang again as he packed up the last of his clothes into the suitcase.

The money had been wired through, and he had just spoken with Louise's consultant to resume the expensive treatment. Louise's cancer was getting worse according to the senior consultant, and she advised that perhaps it was time to move Louise into a medical care centre.

"You mean a hospice?" Douglas had replied in a low growl. "I'll take care of this when I'm back."

"And when are you back to help care for your wife, Mr. Brown?"

"I'm getting ready to travel up now."

"Then we'll discuss when you get here. Our priority is the health of your wife—"

"—and that's my only priority, Mrs. Edmondson."

He ended the call, resumed packing, and Konrad's number buzzed up on the display of his Nokia.

"He got Sanderson! Even with three guards, the son of a bitch got him. In his own house. What chance have I got?"

"Shit! When was this?"

"A few hours ago. It's a bloodbath in there. Sanderson was caught in a fucking beartrap, then butchered with a knife. He's insane, and I'm fucking next."

"Konrad, for crying out loud—you have to submit everything we've found and let the capable officers on your force take him down."

"I know, Douglas, I know. It's over, and I'm probably going to prison—for me, it's over—over—but I want to do one good thing—for you, Douglas. If you'll permit me."

"I need to leave and see Louise."

Konrad ignored him. "The specialists I mentioned. Zurich." Konrad almost sounded breathless, his voice quietening. "The world's best, and she'll have the same treatment and care as a royal family member. Imagine that, huh, Douglas?"

"Please stop, Konrad. This is nothing short of bribery."

Konrad cleared his throat. "Well, we're way past that. You've already taken my money. I've already set it all up ready to go. The appointments for Louise, the money set aside in a separate account that you can access. The instructions in an envelope. I can't guarantee what will happen with her—illness, but she'll have world-class care. The best."

Douglas re-opened his suitcase lid with one hand, staring at the contents, then lifted his glasses onto his forehead and massaged the bridge of his nose.

"What is the plan exactly?"

Chapter 29

Axmed Hamza watched the high street from his car where Konrad Lynch had parked and gone into a café. The late afternoon light had faded to evening, and the dullness was dotted with the artificial glow from shop signs and headlights.

He had followed Lynch, who travelled alone from his home in East Molesey, and waited with a faint smile on his lips. Occasionally he picked at olives and pitta bread from a small lunchbox on the passenger seat and sipped from his water bottle.

The pinnacle of the great mountain had been reached.

The intense investigation in tracking down these men, to smuggling himself into the United Kingdom then preparing his revenge in precise detail had been overwhelming, but he had seen it through. His dead family and those others who had all died at the hands of these men would be waiting for him with open arms and grateful hearts.

All these rich men had deserved to die, hunted like the animals they were, just as they had hunted his family.

Hamza's mind wandered back to the catalyst that brought him to the UK seeking revenge. When Fawzia had become his wife, Hamza began fishing, and thanks to the support of Fawzia's relatives was able to save up to buy his own boat.

For a while, despite the worsening situation on the mainland, Hamza was able to scrape a living. Focus on his family. However, life became a relentless toil with the same long routine every day.

At least we have peace, Hamza kept telling himself, but his frustration grew, nevertheless.

Then, one day, Hamza decided to take his wife and another young couple they had become friends with, Isaaq and his wife Astur, out to one of the islands. Just to do something different and to explore a bit. To have a much-needed break.

They packed up some food, plenty of water and headed out from Jasiirada Chula to find one of the smaller islands and have some leisure time.

Their timing could not have been worse.

Hamza had heard stories about the increase in piracy along the Somalian coast, but they targeted big ships, and it wasn't something he ever thought would involve him.

The motorboat appeared just twenty minutes into their journey and beelined for Hamza's small fishing boat. Isaaq shouted over to him, but Hamza wasn't worried. It must be locals, he thought, and there might be a problem back at their island, and so he slowed down. When the motorboat came closer, and the figures wielded AK-47s, he realised he was mistaken and tried to speed off, but their boat was faster, and gunshots rang out over their heads. Realising the game was up he slowed to a stop, and all four of them held up their hands.

Two of the three armed men, dressed in black fatigues, aimed their weapons at them, while the other hooked the boats together. Then they were ordered aboard. They clambered onto the pirate vessel and were immediately tied up and blindfolded.

Hamza assessed his options but escaping or overpowering them was just not an option. Instead, he tried to reason with them and in return got a gun butt in the side of the face.

The friends sat in silence, praying to Allah. They had no idea why this was happening. Hamza kept quiet too and decided to wait. Their fate, it seemed, was well out of their hands. After an hour's journey, the boat slowed and then came to a stop. Hamza felt the boat being hauled onto a beach, and they were pulled out and frog-marched up onto the island for another twenty minutes. Then they all had their blindfolds and ties removed outside a sizeable concrete hut before being pushed into a squalid, stinking room with another three people.

"What is happening?" Hamza's wife, Fawzia, whimpered.

Hamza tried to comfort her, but she shook with fear, as did their friends. Hamza turned to the others already in the hut. Two men and a woman, in their 20s like them.

"How long have you been here? Do you know what is happening?"

The taller of the men shook his head. "Three-four days. We were taken from our boat."

"Us too," Issaq said.

"We have been treated worse than pigs," the woman said, with contempt.

"Who are they?" Hamza jabbed a thumb outside.

The two men and the woman shook their heads in unison.

"Pirates. Criminals," said one.

"We have been kidnapped that's for certain."

"What could they want with us? It is not like we have rich family who will pay a ransom."

Hamza was jolted from his memory as the familiar figure appeared from the café in a heavy trenchcoat and looked around before moving off on foot down Wimbledon Park Road. Hamza grabbed his bag and got out of his vehicle, following on the opposite side of the road.

Lynch walked past endless semi-detached houses until he reached the edge of Wimbledon Park, then turned and walked through a gate and disappeared into the small car park beyond it.

Hamza tailed him, but the light was fading fast now, and he quickened his pace. He just caught sight of his target's trenchcoat, heading deeper into the park, alongside a hedgerow and wooden fence. Overhead, a pink sky gradient darkened to night, and distant trees were now black shapes on the horizon.

The path curved then opened up parallel to a column of fir trees, and Hamza found himself directly behind his target, the park lake catching the twilight just beyond him.

Then the figure was gone, into the line of trees.

Hamza quickened his pace to a jog, then came to an enclosed oval area and he realised it was an athletics track. He caught movement and saw the glimpse of a familiar face. The private detective who had surprised him in the car park seemed to be holding up a mobile phone. Behind the PI other approaching figures moved towards Hamza.

A surge of metallic pain, spiking his senses, threw him to the ground. The confusion came in waves and Hamza fought against the disorientation, and he realised what was happening.

He had been caught with a stun gun.

Shaking, Hamza wiped drool from his mouth as he looked up at Douglas Brown in a grey trenchcoat, smiling down at him.

"Hello, Hamza."

***

Douglas had finally agreed to help Konrad one more time. He was scraping the barrel when it came to his better judgement, not to mention morals, but money talked and that Zurich consultant was too good to pass. Nothing mattered more to him than the health and life of Louise, and if it meant helping a slimeball like Konrad, then so be it.

At his house in East Molesey, Douglas and Konrad were in his kitchen to plan out the trap.

It was simple enough. Douglas and Konrad were pretty much the same build and weight. For Douglas, it meant dying his hair black and losing the glasses, but if it were just a case of leading Hamza at long distance to a place where he could be grabbed, then it would be good enough.

It was bloody dangerous, of course. Hamza wanted to kill Konrad, the last of the murderous hunters who had killed his family. Konrad himself would stay in the house, armed, with all doors locked. However, with Douglas leading the killer away, there shouldn't be any problems. It would be Douglas in the firing line.

"You sure about this?" Konrad asked, standing over his kitchen table, looking down at the stun gun Douglas planned to use.

"No—can't say I am."

Douglas had gone to the house in the boot of Konrad's car so as not to alert Hamza who was surely keeping watch. From an upstairs window, with binoculars, they had searched for any signs of him but had come up with nothing.

He was there, somewhere, waiting.

"Hazelle in place?" Konrad asked. "Yes and three constables she's recommended."

Konrad shook Douglas's hand.

"Thank you—best of luck Douglas. Be careful, alright?"

Douglas nodded, took the stun gun and placed it in his trench coat pocket.

"I will. See you when it's over."

He walked out of the front door, looked around and got into Konrad's Audi, one of three vehicles at his disposal, but with tinted windows it was perfect. He drove out of the gates, well under the speed limit and cruised towards London. He eyed his rearview mirror but didn't see any noticeable tail.

Relax, thought Douglas. He's good, that's why you can't see him.

After a fifteen-minute drive on the A3, Douglas pulled over just before Wimbledon and watched his side mirror with increasing worry. He took out his phone and called Hazelle.

"I don't think he's following. I haven't seen head nor tail. I know he's good but—"

"All we can do is carry on as planned," Hazelle replied, confidently. "Go to the café. I'm nearby. I'll see if I can see him there."

"Alright. Be careful."

"You too."

Douglas pulled off again and continued down Wimbledon Park Road, looking for a space on the busy street. Finally, he saw one, pulled in and waited for a few minutes.

Still no bloody sign.

He got out and crossed the road to a Starbucks and headed inside. All he could do was buy a coffee as planned and then head to the park. He took his cappuccino and slipped into a seat. His phone beeped inside his coat pocket.

"Hazelle?"

"I see him. He's there in a different car, Douglas. He's got eyes on you."

Douglas felt his heart pace quicken at the words.

"Jesus."

"Are you OK?"

Douglas exhaled a long breath.

"Never better. Alright, Hazelle. Thank you. You go, get into position."

"Be careful, Douglas."

"You too."

***

His hands were sweaty, and he still couldn't quite believe it was over as Hamza grinned back at him from the ground, his arms visibly shaking from the stun shock.

"Hello, Douglas Brown."

111

Douglas frowned. He knew who he was?

There was something else wrong here.

Hamza still didn't seem that surprised that it was him, not Konrad.

Douglas could hear the approaching footfall from Hazelle and the officers coming up behind him. He held his hand up to indicate to them to wait.

"I did my research," Hamza said, gloating. "Always know your enemies. But—you were doing your job—for Konrad—I understand that. I want you to know what those men did, Douglas."

Hamza slowly sat up before continuing. "They used us as prey, human prey, on the island. My wife, friends, myself were let loose on that island to try to run like animals. Pursued by those men with perverted, sick minds to hunt us all down." He paused, spitting on the ground, spittle dribbling from his lips.

"I managed to escape, I found a boat and decided I would hunt every single one of the bastards down. However long it took."

"I know about what happened, truly terrible. Those men deserved to pay for their crimes, but not your way of brutal murder. Public disgrace in the court of law would have sufficed." Douglas said.

"You think men like that would pay for their crimes? Money, Mr. Brown. Money. They would use it like a weapon, so they don't have to face true justice. This way, this was the only way."

He looked up at Douglas.

"Nice show with that disguise but I already knew it was you."

"You knew I wasn't Konrad? Then why did you come?"

Hamza grinned as if he had enjoyed the electrical thunderbolt that Douglas had given him. He pulled himself up onto his knees and with trembling hands held them behind his head.

"My work is done. Vengeance has been served to everyone who murdered and conspired against my family and friends. Now I must pay the price for my sins."

Douglas frowned, confused. "Well, not exactly—murdered or con-spired?"

Then the full horrifying realisation hit him.

Chapter 30

Douglas screeched to a halt outside the property gates and jumped out. They had been left slightly ajar, and he had to push them wider to get through.

Behind him, the distant whoop of sirens.

He ran up the drive towards the dark house, apart from a slither of light from the side door. He made his way towards it, then stopped and paused before moving inside.

The kitchen was quiet, apart from the hum of the fridge. The table they had been sitting at earlier still had the half-empty mugs on it. He hurried across the stone floor to the door and up the stairs to the main hallway. He switched on the lights.

"Konrad?"

No response.

He walked into the study where his old colleague had first introduced him to Hazelle and briefed him on the case. It was empty, so he moved across to the living room. As he switched the light on, he immediately spotted bloody footprints on the carpet.

His heart sank.

Slowly, he padded across the carpet, following the direction they had come, from the adjourning dining room.

It was Konrad's shoes Douglas saw first, as if he was sitting in an armchair, sleeping. Then Douglas moved further in and saw his body, head jerked back, his throat slit wide, with the drained blood having formed a macabre bib on the front of his shirt.

"Jesus!"

Douglas closed his eyes, wishing he hadn't seen this nightmare vision. He had witnessed many crime scenes like this in his career, of course. This one, however, would stay with him for a long time.

He turned away, not looking again and walked back out to the corridor.

As he opened the front door, flashing blue lights from the police cars and ambulance greeted him, and he leaned against the doorframe and waited.

Chapter 31

Douglas sliced a chunk of lemon, placed it in the mug and poured on boiling water. He looked out through the kitchen window, across the rolling fields and cherished the moment of being home. Now all he had to do was focus on Louise, on getting her through the illness. Konrad had made good on his promise that arrangements had been made for premium treatment in Switzerland, should they decide to use it, with the funding coming from a charitable organisation.

Was it ethical? Douglas knew he was fishing in unknown waters when it came to indirectly taking money from a man who had participated, although not actively, in a human hunting horror show.

But when it came to the health of his wife, he would face any consequences if it came to that. The investigation into the whole shitshow still loomed, and Douglas would be answering questions about his part, but that was for another day.

He wondered about Konrad and his inevitable death. Hamza must have been in the house or close by when Douglas was there, heard the whole plan and then murdered Konrad after Douglas left. Whether he would ever find out the truth was another unanswered question that would have to linger.

He took the hot lemon drink into the living room and placed it on the coffee table where Louise, covered in her favourite blanket for comfort, was curled up on the sofa.

"Thank you."

She moved up her feet to make space for Douglas, and he eased himself next to her. Louise picked up her mug and took a sip.

"I'm glad you caught the killer," she said, with pride. "I knew you would."

He nodded and leaned back into the padded sofa.

"When you look at what those men did, well, they deserved it."

"No one deserves to die like that."

"Maybe, maybe not."

"So"—Douglas turned to Lousie—"shall I make that call to the consultant in Zurich?"

Louise put down her mug on the table with a forlorn look.

"I don't know. There must be so many more deserving than me. So many with my cancer that cannot get this super treatment. It's so unfair."

Douglas sighed. "I know, I know. So many sick people cannot get access to the medicines they need—it's insane—but—"

"But?"

"There's an opportunity here," he pleaded, "just a phone call away. It's not a guarantee to cure the cancer, we both know that, but it's the best chance we've got, honey. The best care in the world and—" He stopped and took her hand in his.

"I don't want to lose you. It's a selfish thing."

"Ah, well. Now the truth is revealed, huh?" she said, teasingly.

She squeezed his hand back, and they sat in silence for a few moments as the morning chorus of birdsong drifted through the open window.

The End.

About the Authors

Jay Tinsiano

Jay was born in Ireland but grew up on the flat plains of Lincolnshire surrounded by cows and haystacks before moving to the city of Bristol where he has lived, apart from far-flung nomadic excursions, ever since.

He is the author of the Frank Bowen thriller series, and in collaboration with Jay Newton, the Dark Paradigm Apocalyptic thriller series, Doug Brown and the shorter Dark Ops stories.

Jay is an avid reader, specifically of crime, sci-fi and thrillers with occasional non-fiction thrown in. He can be occasionally found in a Waterstones bookshop café or perhaps a quiet pub furiously scribbling notes and whispering to himself.

Jay Newton

Jay Newton practices and teaches martial arts, is a keen cyclist, manages a band and is an avid fiction reader.

He is currently working on the Dark Paradigm and Dark Ops series with Jay Tinsiano and is co-founder of the Dark Paradigm Publishing imprint.

Jay lives in Bristol, UK with his family

Free Thriller!

Exclusive offer. To grab your FREE Novella eBook (Blood Tide) head to:
https://jaytinsiano.com/secret-access/

PLUS you'll get access to the VIP Jay Tinsiano reading group for:

· Free Books and stories
· Previews and Sneak Peeks
· Exclusive material

Also Available

For a full list of ebook links please visit: jaytinsiano.com

Blood Tide (Doug Brown #1)

Detective Douglas Brown transferred to Hong Kong to forget his past and the dark memory that still haunts him; Richard Blythe.

Blythe, an explosives expert gone rogue, had terrorised London and outwitted Brown, leading to the deaths of countless innocents.

Now the detective's worst fear has come true: Blythe free from prison to wreak havoc and lead Brown in a deadly cat and mouse game in the city of Hong Kong.

Available at all major eBook retailers.
Paperback ISBN: 978-1-9997232-6-2
As a reader, you can get the ebook free at https://jaytinsiano.com/secret-access/

White Horse (Dark Paradigm #1)

Half a world away in Spain and running from his past, a Los Angeles gangster unwittingly takes a train that's headed straight into a terrorist attack. He survives only to face an even deadlier threat.

On that same train: a virologist with clues to a deadly epidemic. Did his secrets die with him in the strike?

Raging in the aftermath, a foul-tempered police chief with a daughter caught in the attack thirsts for revenge. But against whom?

An orphan child without a name disappears down a dark, illegal CIA mind-control programme. Now trained in the ways of death, he prepares to do his master's twisted bidding.

From its first pages, the relentless techno-thriller White Horse drops you with a thunderclap in the middle of these colliding worlds. This tale of global conspiracy that threatens humanity itself will keep you guessing whether anyone can survive.

Available at all major eBook retailers
Paperback ISBN: 978-1-9997232-1-7

Red Horse (Dark Paradigm #2)

Haleema Sheraz, a cyber hacker for the Iranian government, discovers her father has gone missing. Frustrated at the lack of urgency from the police, she investigates and soon reveals a kidnapping network that spans back to Operation Paperclip in World War II.

Meanwhile, her brothers join an ISIS-inspired uprising that is wreaking havoc inside Iran, and finding her father quickly becomes a mission to save her family.

Joe Bowen and Hugo Reese continue to prepare Liberatus for a wider global struggle and find themselves called to help one of their own secret assets-Sirus aka Haleema Sheraz.

Soon they will all be thrust into the battle zone and their lives will change irreversibly in this epic story of bitter struggle against the backdrop of total war.

Available at all major eBook retailers
Paperback ISBN: 978-1-9997232-4-8

False Flag (Frank Bowen #1)

1991: A plan to destabilise Hong Kong is emerging; the key players are being put into place, the wheels are in motion and innocent people will die.

Frank Bowen is a Londoner on holiday in tropical Thailand. Half drunk and strapped for cash, he's the perfect bait for a political plot that will leave him running for his life, with nowhere to turn.

Available at all major eBook retailers
Paperback ISBN: 978-1-9997232-2-4

Pandora Red (Frank Bowen #2)

Frank Bowen's mission is to find a GCHQ whistleblower but in doing so unwittingly risks everything, including his own family's safety.

As part of a covert team, assigned to dangerous missions, Bowen believes he knows what he's up against until a team of Russian mercenaries are thrown into the mix, leaving everyone and everything hanging in the balance.

It's a race against the clock to save all that he holds dear and uncover the dark truths behind his mission.

Available at all major eBook retailers.
Paperback ISBN: 978-1-9997232-3-1

Ghost Order (Frank Bowen #3)

Frank Bowen attempts to piece together a fractured life at home but finds himself pulled back into the dark state once again.

Only, this time, he's playing both sides.

Hired by John Rhodes, founding father of the Liberatus movement, his mission is to escort a valuable asset to South America. Then the spectre of Carl Paterson emerges and Frank finds he has to work once again with his old agency, Ghost 13.

Later, in the depths of the Colombian Darien Gap jungle – swarming with narcos, paramilitary groups and bandits – Frank finds death and evil wait around every corner in the most inhospitable place on earth.

Available at all major eBook retailers.

Paperback ISBN: 978-1-9162397-0-8

Lightning Source UK Ltd.
Milton Keynes UK
UKHW040252150421
382009UK00001B/134